ONE-DOG MAN

One-Dog Man

AHMAD KAMAL

toExcel

San Jose New York Lincoln Shanghai

One-Dog Man

Published by toExcel
an imprint of iUniverse.com, Inc.

For information address:
iUniverse.com, Inc.
620 North 48th Street
Suite 201
Lincoln, NE 68504-3467
www.iuniverse.com

ISBN: 0-595-00990-5

Printed in the United States of America

Tura, this is for you —
MY NEWBORN DAUGHTER.
GROW IN THE IMAGE OF AMINA,
YOUR MOTHER.
BECOME EQUALLY DESIRABLE
AND MAKE SOMEONE, SOMEDAY,
EQUALLY BLESSED...

CONTENTS

		PAGE
1.	Half-Pound Pup	3
2.	Soap	8
3.	Wipazhazha!	25
4.	Adding Machines	29
5.	Spring	35
6.	Paderewski	36
7.	*The Saturday Evening Post*	52
8.	Money	70
9.	Crime Wave	80
10.	Drat!	89
11.	Randolph	106
12.	Beauty and the Beast	137
13.	The End of Youth	162
14.	Desperation	183
15.	Runaway	188
16.	Love	206
17.	For Ever and Ever, Amen	208

vii

ONE-DOG MAN

Half=Pound Pup

JUST the other day a friend gave us a pup—a runt with short legs and champion ancestors and more courage than sense. He wasn't short on sense—just long on courage.

I wasn't home when he arrived. He met me. The front door was open. I stopped the car and got out. A square pup staggered out of the house and sneered at me. I put a foot on the grass and he fell off the steps and started for me, hair erect all down his spine, ears laid back: a half-pound of dog in a towering rage.

The half-pound had gotten hold of my trouser cuff and was knocking himself out trying to rip it off when Amina came out. She's a pretty girl. We've been married going on nine years. She laughed. I asked her.

"Whose is he?"

"Ours . . ."

"Ours?" I asked. "How come? Where'd we get him?"

"Oswald and Oxana brought him over. They'd promised me a pup from the next litter. There he is. He'll grow big."

He was still fighting my trouser cuff. It was *his* grass he defended. I bent down, put one hand under him, disengaged his teeth with the other, and picked him up. He used his milk teeth on my finger. The finger didn't come off and it didn't fight back. The pup stopped struggling and took a look at me.

We studied each other while I went on into the house. His hair rose as I kissed Amina. I sat down and put him in front of me on my knee. He squared off, took a long sidewise look at me, sneered, and charged. He charged over my leg, across my lap, and up the front of me. Then, unable to advance farther, he lunged at my necktie. Dangling, he uttered horrid little roars and shook like fury.

I couldn't help but like him, square body and all. In the next couple of days we saw a lot of each other. He got so that he let me alone and charged others.

He charged the neighbor's cat. She didn't take him seriously; but she walloped him across the nose, just to give him a taste of what she could do. He stopped, backed away, sat down, groaned, licked the blood off his nose, and attacked again. The cat hit him again, harder, arching, outraged. Amina yelled to get him before the cat killed him, or blinded him, or something!

He fought through and got her by the leg. Furious, she

hit him a cuff that spun him around. She was all claws. He licked his chopped-up nose, located the cat through his tears, and waded in.

She ran just as I got there. He'd won, but he was a sight.

I took him in the house and into the bathroom and sat him in the wash basin and put his nose together. He didn't whimper and he didn't complain when I hurt him. He just sat there growling to himself and trying to look at the point of his nose, three-eighths of an inch square of black hamburger.

I had to admire him, but somehow we couldn't get to love each other. I'd be writing and look up and he'd be there, in the far corner of the room, watching me. He didn't come close, just stood off at long-range on his squat little legs, cocked his head this way and that, and looked. We both of us were curious about the other. There was curiosity, but there wasn't affection. Amina saw it.

"Please," she said on the fourth or fifth day, "please let's keep him."

"He's yours," I told her, and grabbed him and put him out before he made a puddle. "He's all yours. If you want him, we'll keep him."

"He's brave."

"He's that all right," I admitted.

We stood by the window and watched him.

"But you don't like him?"

"I like him all right," I said. "He's a good dog. I'm prejudiced against blue bloods. When I was a kid I had a mongrel; but for a pup with ancestors, this one's all right. He doesn't look like much. That's in his favor. I'm not used to dogs that look like much."

"You won't all of a sudden give him away—like last time?"

He'd discovered a mockingbird in a tree and was daring it to come down and fight.

I looked at Amina and told her: "Not if you think that much of him. He stays."

"Think maybe you'll learn to like him?"

"Maybe . . ."

He'd started to dig up some flowers. Amina flew out and got him. She picked him up and brought him back inside.

We went for about a week in the same status. The pup grew to about a pound. When he wasn't following Amina around, he sat in a corner of my work room and watched me type. I'd never seen a pup that could sit still so long. He was something of a distraction. You can never quite tell if a pup is sitting down for resting purposes.

One day Amina came in and saw us there, looking at each other. She laughed at us and the pup gave her a quick, radiant glance. Then he sobered and turned again to me.

Then, at dinner, Amina began again. We had finished eating when she picked him off the floor and sat him in my

lap. He and I took another long and critical stare at each
other. I felt his nose. It had healed almost as good as new.
He sneezed.

"He's nice," she said.

"He's okay," I said.

"Why don't you like him as much as I do?" she asked.
"Why don't you give him a chance?"

It's like this. The pup can stay. I think he's charming.
If she loves him, I'll cherish him. But I can't love another
dog. Not as long as I remember Randolph.

I guess I'm just a one-dog man.

✖✖ 2 ✖✖

Soap

MY CHILDHOOD, up to my ninth year, was curious and wonderful. It was spent on one Indian reservation and then another. Then, quite abruptly, we called a halt to our wandering.

We came to a standstill in Cleveland, on Lake Shore Boulevard, somewhere near the Euclid Beach amusement park, on Lake Erie. My mother settled down to correlate the folklore and legends she'd gathered. I had a week of freedom before school started, but I mooned around the house, homesick for the reservation in the Black Hills where I'd spent the most recent, and therefore the most marvelous, year of my life.

My mother was putting the place in order. I suppose I bothered her. I was trying to. Maybe I depressed her. I was trying that, too. On the afternoon of our second day in Cleveland, she suggested that I go out and make some new friends.

SOAP

"I don't want to," I said. "I don't want *new* friends! I'd like to keep my *old* friends!"

She looked at me.

"Well, I would . . ." I said. "I wanta go back an' see Joey Longtree an' Buddy Lamb an' Mary Heaven. *I don't want any new friends.*"

"Out!" my mother ordered, getting sadder, but firmer.

So I went.

I walked down to the boulevard and stood under a chinaberry tree and watched the traffic whiz past. I stood in the entrance to a filling station on the corner until somebody yelled for me to get out of the way before I got run over.

Then I raced automobiles. There was an old Indian chief; he promised that if I beat the automobiles he'd give me any wish I'd make; anything at all. I said I wanted to go back to the reservation and Mary Heaven. The Indian chief agreed. But I had to win. If I lost I would be electrocuted! I said okay.

I had to get on the mark, a crack in the sidewalk, and watch over my shoulder for a car to cross the intersection. The old Indian chief would say *go* and I'd have to beat the automobile to the nearest telegraph pole.

I didn't accept every challenge. There were rules to be abided by. I recited:

"Chikasaw, Choctaw, Cherokee, *Cree* . . ."

Go! the chief shouted. *Run!* The first automobile after *Cree* was my adversary.

9

I won!

"Arapaho, Papago, Huron, *Hopi* . . ."

I ran again, and lost . . .

"Shawnee, Pawnee, Sioux, *Apache* . . ."

I gritted my teeth. I'd lost again. I got 'on the mark, desperate.

"Iroquois, Zuni, Pima, *Yaqui* . . ."

I won, barely.

I won about half the time, and lost the other half, which didn't decide anything. The Indian chief was frowning. To get my wish I'd have to show a clear-cut victory. I wanted with all my heart to go back to Mary Heaven. So I cheated.

"Seneca, *Shoshone* . . ." I ran, looking over my shoulder, guilty, but certain of victory.

I ran smack into a letter box fastened to a lamppost.

I caught it over my right eye. There was a flash of bright light and then I banged the other side of my head against the sidewalk. I sat up and the man came out of the filling station and said would I *please* go away, that he couldn't have anybody committing suicide in front of his place. It was bad for his business.

I held my head.

"Hey," the man said, concerned, "you hurt bad?"

"No!" I said.

"Lemme see," he said.

"I hate this town!" I said, fighting back the tears.

He helped me up off the sidewalk and led me into the filling station.

"Sit down there, on the stool," he said. "We better do something about that eye. You got a big lump over it." He got some ice out of the tank under the water cooler and put it on my eye. I flinched. "Go ahead," he said, "cry—if you want to. I got some kids about your age. They'd sure cry."

"I don't wanta," I said, lying.

"Racin' cars, huh?" he asked, changing the subject. "What you get when you won?"

"How'd you know?" I asked.

"Everybody does," he said.

"Sure enough?"

"Sure."

"I got to go back. An Indian chief sent me," I said. "When I lost I was electrocuted. I had it comin' to me, I cheated. I was supposed to wait for 'Mohawk, *Seminole . . .'*"

"Got to go back where?"

"South Dakota," I said.

"That where you're from?"

"Yes," I said, "right now." I pressed the ice against my eye. "An' I wanta go back!"

"You're the kid moved in just down the street."

"Round the corner—green house," I said. "The ugly house. I *hate* this place! How'd you know?"

"Little girl told me," the man said. "She knows everything. She's engaged to my boy."

"Little girl?"

"Four years old," the man said. "He's four and a half."

"I'm engaged . . ." I said. "*I hate this place!*"

"I believe you," he said, nodding. "Where's she?"

"Back in South Dakota," I said, feeling my eye. "On the reservation. We're gonna get married just as soon as I'm earnin' enough money to support us. Gosh, my eye!"

"From the mouths of babes . . ." the man said.

"I beg pardon?" I asked.

"You got a proper eye, all right," he said, not explaining. "What's her name? You say she's on a reservation, how come?" He got another hunk of ice for my eye; the first had melted.

"Mary . . ." I said. "Mary Heaven. She's Indian. Sioux. She cried when we had to say good-bye. We went for a long hike in the wheat. She gave me Gabriel."

"Who's Gabriel?"

"He died on the way here," I explained, saddened. "He got sick on some tomatoes. He was a hawk. Hawks aren't supposed to eat vegetables."

"I didn't know Indians cried," the man said, playing with the cash register. "I always read they didn't."

"They do," I said. "They're humans, just like other kids. Hasn't she got a pretty name?"

"*She has!*" he said, ringing up NO SALE, then closing the

12

drawer again. *"Mary Heaven.* She certainly has. You
should be very happy."

"I'm not," I said. "I'm sad."

"Yes," he said, "I can see that."

"You're laughin' at me," I accused, stiffening.

"No!" he denied, serious. "Cross my heart!"

"I thought you were," I said.

"I wasn't. How's your eye?"

"Much better, thank you."

"How old're you? Eleven?"

"I'm goin' on nine," I said. "Do I look eleven?"

"I thought you were. What were you doing on a reservation?"

"I wasn't doin' much," I admitted, feeling the other
side of my head, where I'd connected with the sidewalk.
He felt of it too. I said, "My mother was gettin' folklore
an' things from the Indians. You should see the mosquitoes
out there!"

"Head's all right on this side," he said. "Got a bump,
but nothing bad. The walk was flat. It was the edge of
the letter box did the damage. How long were you there?
You aren't from Dakota?"

"More'n a year," I said. *"South* Dakota. There's two.
Before that we were in Arizona an' New Mexico an'
Florida an' all over the place. How'd you know?"

"You talk like a Southern boy. What's your daddy do?
How come your mother travels so much?"

"We don't travel much," I said, feeling vaguely uncomfortable. "We just go places and stop a while. He's a big man. More'n six feet. He weighs two hundred pounds an' then some. He's very firm with me. But very kind. She writes reports an' stuff about Indians. I had a sister. She died when I was little. I don't remember her very well. She caught the measles from me. Measles are very dangerous when you're twenty-three. That's when she died. I was more sorry when Gabriel died . . ."

"You don't have to tell me things you don't want to," the man said, interrupting.

"I don't mind," I said. "I'm not a Southern boy, I'm a Westerner. I was born in Colorado . . ." I lowered my eyes, blurted: "I lied just now about my father. I never knew him. He died when I was a baby. I always lie when people ask me questions."

"Me, too," the man said.

"The rest was truth," I said, feeling better. "I can speak all kinds of Indian languages. They're the nicest people I ever met. I gotta go now."

"Yeah," the man said. "I got some things to do around here myself. Drop around any time. You'll meet my kids in the neighborhood. You'll like them."

An automobile rolled up to the pumps.

"Good-bye," I said.

"So long," he said. "Watch out for letter boxes."

I cut across an empty lot and went down another street. I wasn't feeling so strange any more. Cleveland was getting a little more human. I walked as tall as I could—to look more like eleven.

>※※※<

Then I met Babe. He was hunkered down by the trunk of a big elm, intent upon something between his toes.

"Hello, little boy," I said. "Whatcha got?"

He looked up. He had yellow hair and a dirty face.

"Who're you?" he asked, scowling.

"I just moved here," I explained. "From South Dakota. Before that I lived in Gallup an' Tucson an' Fort Myers an' Miami, an' that's not all. How old're you?"

"Five," he said, still squatting there. "You?"

"I look eleven," I said, "but I'm goin' on nine. Whatcha got?"

"Worm."

"What you doin' with it?"

"Spittin' on ut." He turned back to his previous employment, closing the conversation.

"Why?"

"G'wan, get away f'm me!" he warned, turning his back to me and frowning up over his shoulder. "Ya touch me an' I'll yell fer my big brothers!"

"What's eatin' you?" I asked.

"G'wan, *I'll yell*," he threatened.

I looked around.

"I'm not scared of anybody's brothers," I said. "How old're they?"

"Bigger'n you, anyways!" he said in a shout. "*I'll yell fer 'em!*"

"Where d'you live?" I asked, just to be on the safe side.

"*Right there,*" he shrieked, "*in that there house!*" We were right in front of it, a gray house, small, and old-fashioned. "My name's Babe. *Get away f'm me!*"

"I'm not hurtin' ya," I said. "Nutty!"

"Ain't gonna, neither! Nutty, yerself . . ."

"Lemme see the worm," I insisted; it wasn't only the worm, it was the principle of the thing.

"*No!*" he shrieked.

"Why not?"

At that moment two boys came out from behind the house. Twins.

"Whatcha doin' ta him?" one demanded of me. They advanced menacingly. "What's he been doin' ta ya, Babe?"

"Pushin' me," Babe lied, getting behind them. "He wants my worm!"

"Horse feathers!" I said. "I didn't touch him. Button head! What'd I do with a spit-covered caterpillar?"

"He jus' moved here," Babe said to the twins. "Hear what he said? Callin' me names!"

"Where from?" one of the twins demanded.

"What's it to ya?" I said, deciding not to run. "We came from South Dakota, on th' Indian reservation. What's it to ya?"

"Indians? What kinda Indians? Coppery Indians?"

I'd put a fallen leaf on my shoulder. So had one of the twins, the one who hadn't said anything. We stood there with our chins stuck out.

"Comanche Indians?" the interested twin demanded. "Utes? Chippewas? Algonkins? Cheyennes?"

"Sioux Indians," I said. "*Everybody* knows Sioux Indians live in South Dakota. How old're you guys? Where'd you learn so many Indian tribes?"

"Sock 'im!" Babe yelled, furious at the delay.

"Shut up," the talkative twin told him. He turned back to me. I kept my eyes on the silent twin, the immediate danger. The other one said: "We learned about Indians in school; we studied 'em. We got our own private collection of flint arrowheads. Our uncle's got a farm. We're goin' on ten. *You* ever see any Indians? *You* an *Indian?*"

"Uh-uh," I said. "I'm an American. Sure I saw Indians. I *speak* Indian! I got a peace pipe an' a war axe."

"Clunk 'im!" Babe screamed. "Why don' ya sock 'im? Whatcha scared of?"

They ignored him. The silent twin said: "Say somethin' in Indian."

"What kind?" I asked. "I speak all kinds—Sioux, Iroquois, Papago, Apache, Seminole. Any kind."

"The first kind."

"Wipazhazha!"

"What's 'at?" the silent one asked, taking the chip off his shoulder.

"Soap," I said, throwing my chip away.

"Holy smoke!" the other one said. "They got soap, too? I thought they was wild savages!"

"Sure they got soap!" I said. I was thinking of Mary Heaven's shining face. "They smell of soap. They're just the same as us—only they got more mosquitoes. They got so many mosquitoes out there, I used to run up an' down wavin' my arms an' yellin'."

"That chase 'em off?"

"No," I admitted, "but I had to."

"Look," one of the twins sad, the silent one, "I'm Bob. You wanta be friends?"

"You wanta belong to our secret society?" the other twin continued. "Jus' us two belong now. We got a swell clubhouse dug in th' field over yonder. I'm James. Our name's Scott."

"Sure," I said. "I'm gonna live here."

"Ever goin' back?" Babe asked. He'd given up hope for a fight.

"Course I'm goin' back!" I said. "I'm engaged to be married to a girl named Mary Heaven. She's waitin'. She's Indian, prettier'n a picture."

"C'mon in th' house," James said. "You gotta meet our Mom!"

We went in the back door. Mrs. Scott was in the kitchen.

"Mom," James said, introducing me, "he's our new friend. He jus' come from North Dakota on th' Indian reservation an' he can speak it!"

"*South* Dakota . . ." I corrected. "Sioux Indians. Pleased to meet you."

"Well, hello," Mrs. Scott said. She was big all over and had beautiful white hands. "You're the new little boy. I heard a new boy'd moved into the neighborhood. Sit down and have some milk and cookies. Who hit you in the eye? One of my boys?" She looked at them sternly.

"We didn' fight him," James said quickly. "Them Coffees musta got him. We sure didn't!"

"No'm," I agreed. "I ran into a letter box. Who're the Coffees?"

"Some guys . . ." Bob said, and let it go at that.

"Letter box?" Babe sniffed, disbelieving.

"Who tol' you about him, Mom?" James asked, ignoring his kid brother.

Mrs. Scott smiled and looked at Babe.

"Babe's girl," she said. Babe simpered and twisted and finally fell over his own foot. Mrs. Scott turned to me. "She lives right down the block from you. A little girl. Her name's Myrtle."

"Yes'm," I said. "I guess I saw her around a couple times. I really ran into a letter box. Your dad—I mean their dad—Mister Scott, he's the man in the gas station, isn't he?"

"How'd you know?" Bob asked me.

"He's a very good friend of mine," I said.

"Say somethin' in Indian," James insisted, "so's Mom can hear."

"What'll I say?"

"Say 'soap' again," Bob prompted.

"Wipazhazha," I said. "That's 'soap' in Sioux."

"Say 'soap' in somethin' else!" Babe demanded.

"He's a troublemaker," James apologized. "Tha's why we won't let him be a member of th' secret society. Not till he grows up a couple years. Don't pay no attention ta him."

"No," Bob agreed.

"I don't mind," I said. I said 'soap' in Iroquois, Papago, Apache, Seminole, and Navajo:

"Savǫ!

ßavon!

ßawón!

Sōp!

Tqalawhush! . ."

Babe sat down on the alcove bench, beside me. He grinned when I looked at him; he was satisfied. We all had cookies and milk and were still sitting there, talking about Indians, when Mr. Scott came home. He said hello very loud when he saw me there with his boys. He said he was glad that I'd met his family. He told Mrs. Scott that he and I were very good friends; just as I'd said. Then he took a good look at me and said that I'd sure developed a genuine hundred-dollar shiner!

"He run inta a mail box?" Babe asked.

"I picked him up," Mr. Scott said. "I saw him do it." He turned to me. "You tell them about Gabriel yet?"

"No, sir," I shook my head. "Not yet."

"Tell them," he said, sitting down with us and taking Babe onto his lap to make room. "I've been thinking about Gabriel."

"He was my hawk," I explained to the others. "He died when we were drivin' here from South Dakota. Mary Heaven—the girl I'm gonna marry—gave him to me when I was goin' away—to remember her by. . . ."

"A honest-ta-gosh hawk?" Babe interrupted.

Mrs. Scott was busy at the kitchen sink.

"Leave that and come sit here with us," Mr. Scott said to his wife. "Listen to this—"

"Mary Heaven. What a pretty name!" Mrs. Scott said, doing as he told her. She was drying her hands.

"That's *her* name," I said, "not the hawk's. His name was Gabriel. Mary Heaven gave him to me. She's Indian. She's beautiful."

"Yeah, yeah," Bob said, impatient. "Tell us about th' hawk, Gabriel."

"We caught him when he was a baby," I said, "a little teensy, fluffy powder-puff with black eyes an' beak an' strong red legs. I got him out of the nest—in a big cottonwood tree. It was so high up, if I'd slipped and fallen I'd sure splashed when I lit, just like a paper bag fulla water!"

"Gracious!" Mrs. Scott said. Mr. Scott and the boys smiled at her discomfort.

"What kinda tree?" Babe asked. "Who named him?"

"Shut up!" the twins said.

"Leave him alone, you two!" Mrs. Scott said.

"Go ahead with your story, son," Mr. Scott said.

"Cottonwood," I said. "Great big trees. They don't grow around here. Mary Heaven named him, because she loved him so. An' because he had wings . . ."

"Isn't that great!" Mr. Scott said to Mrs. Scott. "Mary Heaven named a hawk Gabriel. I like that!"

"Aw, *Pop!*" the twins protested.

"Go ahead, I'll be quiet," Mr. Scott said to me.

"Well," I went on, "we fed him an' took good care of him an' he grew up. All the white fluff fell out an' he got lovely speckled feathers an' stood up straight an' proud on our fingers, like a little human being. He was awful proud. Then, all of a sudden, he got so's he'd notice when other birds flew around. It made him nervous. He'd move his head, sudden, watching them; then he'd scream, real angry.

"Look at my finger—where he bit a hunk out." I showed it to them. "He bit Mary Heaven worse. He didn't mean to. He just got excited an' tried to sharpen his beak on our fingers like they were twigs.

"We were just beginnin' to teach him to catch doves, when I had to go away. He was handsome . . ."

"What happened ta him?" Babe asked.

"He died on the way here," I said, sadly. "We went in a hamburger stand an' left him perched on the radiator cap an' some dopey dame gave him some tomato. Hawks don't dare eat anythin' else but meat, raw meat. Gabriel was young an' didn't know any better. He passed away a couple hours later. We stopped down the road an' I buried him in a meadow."

Babe put his head down on his arms and burst into tears.

"I'm sorry," I apologized to Mr. and Mrs. Scott. "I didn't mean to make anybody cry." I was kind of misty-eyed myself.

"That's all right," Mr. Scott said, patting Babe on the head. "Everybody's got to cry seventy-four gallons before they grow up, and another seventy-four after they get their growth. It won't hurt him any."

"I never seen a grown man cry," James said, rubbing his eyes.

"No," Mr. Scott said. "The tears drip down inside."

"Well!" Mrs. Scott said, drawing a deep sigh.

"You got a dog?" I asked.

"Uh-uh," Bob said. "We had one when we was kids like Babe."

"Her name was Teddy," James continued. "She got run over by a motorcycle."

"Dear," Mrs. Scott said, "whatever got us started on so much unhappiness?"

"Gonna get another?" I asked.

The twins looked at their father and mother.

"I'd kinda like to have a pup," I said. "Maybe we could have one together?"

Mr. Scott looked at the boys, serious.

"Huh, Pop?" Babe asked, wiping away his tears.

"*William!*" Mrs. Scott said, shaking her head. He didn't pay any attention.

"All right!" he said suddenly. "But *you* kids're going to *take care* of him this time! *You've* got to earn him *yourself.* He's *your* responsibility!"

"He's got to be a *boy*-dog!" Mrs. Scott said anxiously. "I'm not going through that again!" Mr. Scott nodded and added: "A *boy*-dog!"

Babe laughed. The twins grinned. They became excited.

"We'll all three of us own him!" James said to me. "He'll belong ta th' secret society . . ."

"What about me?" Babe wailed.

"Le's let him into the society—an' no more members, ever!" I suggested. "We can't split one pup more'n four ways."

"You got any brothers or sisters?" Bob asked cautiously.

"Uh-uh . . ." I said.

Then Babe put his hand in mine.

All of a sudden I loved Cleveland very dearly.

$$\text{>>>> } 3 \text{ <<<<}$$

Wipazhazha!

T H E two Coffee boys were about the orneriest kids
that ever lived. They roamed around full of energy
and looking for trouble. They had their own private clubhouse up in a tree and sporadically went out on raids and
busted up every other clubhouse in the neighborhood.
They sassed grown-ups, flung rocks at dogs, threw cats
into incinerators, and picked fights with everybody. They
beat up little kids; they beat up kids their own size; and
they ganged up on bigger kids. They weren't particular.

I learned a lot about them in my first few months in
Cleveland. The Coffees had always been especially mad at
James and Bob because of the indestructible clubhouse
they'd dug. A hole in the ground couldn't satisfactorily be
torn up. They could chuck dead cats in it, garbage, tin
cans, broken bottles—all of which we could, and did, re-
move with a moment's effort. The clubhouse would be

just as good as new. It was even better. Its history was enriched by each attack it survived; its fame spread.

After my admission to the secret society, making me the third member privileged to use the clubhouse, Babe the fourth, the enmity between the Coffee tree house and our dugout became even more intense. The fights became more bitter. No quarter was asked—and none given. In all innocence I'd added considerable glamour to our secret society. James and Bob and I would summon one another across the school yard, or street, or wherever we were, sometimes blocks and blocks apart, with mystic and piercing cries such as *Wipazhazha!* or *Tqalawhush!* or *Savon!* and other sounds meaning the same thing. Words which, all being "soap" in their respective tribal tongues, possibly hadn't ever been uttered in Ohio before, even in the day of the red man. Chances are that soap, with fire-water, gunpowder, and grand larceny, came in with the savage and unpredictable Anglo-Saxon.

One day Miss Roth, our teacher, heard us yell the secret summons across the school yard, and reported us to Mr. Eddy, the principal, for using obscene language. Mr. Eddy demanded to know what we'd said. We told him Wipazhazha, but we wouldn't tell what it meant. That would have robbed it of its magic. All three of us were punished. After that we went around whispering the word to one another. Soap. *Soap.* SOAP. *SOAP.* It was wonderful.

Once, on a Saturday afternoon, before it got too cold to

swim, the Coffees caught us in the creek on the other side
of the amusement park. We didn't see them until it was
too late. The other kids got out in time, running out of
the water, grabbing their clothes, and racing off through
the poison ivy.

"*WIPAZHAZHAZHAZHA!*" Babe yelled, suddenly
aware of what was happening. He'd been sitting in the
shallows. He couldn't swim. He splashed up on the bank
and disappeared into the poison ivy, naked, like the
others.

We, the twins and I, trod water and looked around in
alarm. Then we saw the Coffee boys.

"Gotcha!" the bigger of the two said. He was Bert.

"We gotcha good!" the other one said. He was Jimmy.
Both of them shook fists at us. We paddled around, dog-
fashion, trying to figure out what to do. Our clothes were
on the Coffee bank.

"Come on out an' get licked," Bert challenged, grinning in anticipation.

Then Jimmy found our clothes.

"Hey," he said to Bert, "looka here. Le's us take their
stuff up by the highway an' throw it up in a tree. How
about it?"

"Rub everythin' in th' mud, first," Bert suggested.

Jimmy pushed Babe's clothes into a mud hole and
stomped on them.

"*Pazhazhazhazha!*" Babe shrilled from somewhere in
the poison ivy; he was watching.

27

"C'mon," Bob said, making for the bank. "TQALA-WHUSH!"

So we went up on the bank and got beat up.

>≫≫≪≪

I learned a lot from the twins. They worked on the principle that a guy could get hurt only just so badly—and no worse. And they'd already suffered that much on four or five occasions, and hadn't perished. So mere pain held no terror for them. We were beaten that day at the swimming hole, but the Coffees retreated. We saved our clothes.

I think that Bert and Jimmy didn't really hate us as much as we believed. Maybe they just wanted to find out what Wipazhazha meant—and didn't know how to go about it.

And we wanted to be friends with them. They had a cute little girl-dog named Dora. The twins said she had pups regularly. We wanted one of her next litter. It looked as if we might have to wait until Spring for our pup. None of the dogs in the neighborhood seemed to be in love.

✖✖✖ 4 ✖✖✖

Adding Machines

MAYBE I could say "soap" in Sioux, Iroquois, Papago, Apache, Navajo, and Seminole; and Hopi and Osage too, if I strained myself, but long division and the decimal point took me into a cold sweat. I had a mental block, sort of an air-tight, burglar-proof, chrome-steel door in my head—and it swung shut whenever numbers were involved.

A blackboard full of problems to solve had, on one occasion, even made me forget my name. I didn't tell anybody. I just sat there at my desk as though I knew it. After a while it came back to me.

I'd been on every Indian reservation in North America—barring three or four—but had never gone to school, one school, for a whole semester. It almost killed me.

I could swim and shoot and knock pigeons out of the air with a sling shot, but I hated teamwork and organized recreation and physical culture. I could lie out in Mentor Marsh for hours, waiting for a turtle to come far enough out of the water so that I could grab him, or waiting for a sparrow hawk to pounce on one of my snares; but I couldn't sit still in a classroom.

Somehow I got into fights during every recess. I got into fights before class, during fire drill, at lunch hour, and on the way home. So did the twins. They weren't so hot in arithmetic either.

"Dear, dear, dear," Miss Roth said after school one day. The twins and I had been kept in. "Your mothers must've been frightened by adding machines."

"I beg pardon," I said, thinking perhaps that I'd missed something, and trying to ingratiate myself.

"Never mind, never mind," Miss Roth said, moving some papers on her desk.

"Okay," James said.

Miss Roth looked at him and compressed her lips.

"I don't appreciate insolence!" she said. "Haven't you a low enough mark in deportment?"

"Gosh, Miss Roth . . ." James protested. "I was jus' tryin' ta be agreeable. If you think I'm insolent, wait till Babe, our kid brother, starts school!"

"I can hardly wait!" Miss Roth said, looking out of the window.

"Me, too," James said.

"That's quite enough!" Miss Roth said.

It was snowing outside, the last watery blizzard of the winter. Miss Roth sat back in her chair and relaxed. Her face sagged ever so slightly. The steam radiators muttered. The janitor was banking the fires for the night.

"Tell me," Miss Roth said, still looking out into the whiteness, "what is there about arithmetic, and being little gentlemen, that you can't grasp?"

There was a moment's silence. The clock ticked. It was three forty-five. The corridors were silent. We should have been out at three fifteen.

"Speakin' ta us?" James asked.

"Is there anyone else in the room?" Miss Roth snapped, her jaw getting a little firmer. She pivoted her chair and faced us. James looked around the room.

"No'm," he admitted, all innocence, "not unless they're hidin' under a desk somewhere. I'll look . . ."

Miss Roth froze him with her eyes, but it seemed to me that her lips twitched as though they wanted to laugh.

"*You!*" she said, pointing to Bob. He jumped in his seat. "Say something!"

"What?" he asked, breathless at the sudden onslaught.

"Anything at all," Miss Roth said, more gently now. "Perhaps if once in a while you'd say something, I could find out what's wrong with you."

"I feel fine," Bob reassured her. "I jus' wanta go home."

"Why don't you do better in arithmetic?"

"I don't like it," Bob said, smiling and sincere. He had a wonderful smile.

"But you must learn to like it!" Miss Roth exclaimed, overwhelmed by his candor. "Robert, you really *must!* Otherwise you'll never amount to anything."

"Yes'm," Bob said.

"Yes, what?" she insisted.

"Yes, he'll never amount ta anythin'," James said. "Me, either."

Miss Roth ignored him. She kept after Bob, asked: "What do you want to do when you grow up? Tell me . . ."

"Hunt, an' trap . . ." Bob said uncomfortably, but confidently. "An' breed champion dogs an' horses!" That's what he wanted.

"An' fight a war," James added, "tat-tat-tat-tat-tat . . . We'll do that first."

They fought in a war all right. They did it first, just as James said they would. They never got around to the dogs and horses. They died over Germany, the Third Reich, together, both in the same bomber.

Miss Roth turned to me.

"I'm goin' back to South Dakota," I said, anticipating her. "I'm gonna get Mary Heaven an' we're gonna get married. Then I'll be a lawyer. Then a judge. Then Supreme Court judge. Then President!"

Miss Roth threw up her hands.

"Go home, please," she said. "Go home immediately!"

><><><

The ice on Lake Erie and on the creeks and ponds had begun to get dangerous. Spring was just around the corner.

The Saturday after Miss Roth kept us in, Jerry Rice

fell through the ice and got drowned. On the day of the funeral I saw the first robin of the new season. We were in Jerry's house; his mother had seen us outside and called us in. She thought we wanted to see him. We didn't. We were just passing by.

The hall and parlor smelled of incense and flowers. We took off our caps. A man showed us the way to where the coffin was. It was covered with lilies and lined with satin and there were candles burning.

We filed past and looked at Jerry's waxen forehead and rosy cheeks.

"Gee, don' he look nacheral?" George Hopper whispered as we walked past the coffin. George was in our class in school.

"Yeah," we whispered.

"I never seen nobody dead before," James whispered.

"I jus' seen a robin red-breast outside the window," I whispered.

"Dogs'll be havin' pups pretty soon," Bob whispered.

We got out in a hurry. George Hopper hung around to look at Jerry some more.

"Hey," James said just as soon as we were outside, "you guys see what they done ta him! He was all made up like a girl. Even lipstick!"

"Dogs'll be havin' pups pretty soon. They always do in th' Spring," Bob said.

"You already said that," I said. I took a good look at him. "You're awful white!"

"Where's the robin red-breast?" James asked.

"It was over there in the chinaberry tree," I said. Then I belched.

"I'm gonna be sick," Bob said.

"Le's get away from Jerry's house," James said.

"What'd she make us come in for?" I asked. "He didn' even go to our school. He was Catholic. He went to the parochial school."

"I beat him up once," James said. "He thought he was tough. I wish I hadn't."

We got around the corner. Then, suddenly, all three of us were sick on the sidewalk.

>>>< 5 ><<<

$\mathcal{S}pring$

O N T H E following Saturday we went out to Mentor Marsh and built ourselves a boat. It had a galvanised-iron bottom, a packing-case hull, and board oars. We nailed it together with a brick. But it floated.

Every Saturday after that we went out there to relax. We'd ditch Babe, hitch-hike the twenty-five miles out to the marsh, drag the four-cornered boat out of its hiding place in the cattails, empty the water out, and paddle out into the swamp to fish for bullheads and snapping turtles. For a couple of weeks we didn't get a single bite. They were still down in the mud where they'd slept all winter. We didn't mind. We just floated around. The packing case turned over easily. We didn't talk much. We had to concentrate.

The twins never did talk very much. They used telepathy. Then I got so that I could use it too. It came to me one day out there in the packing case.

✕✕✕ 6 ✕✕✕

Paderewski

SUMMER vacation came just in time. In fact it came about a week too late. We had music trouble.

Up to a certain age, boys—average, ordinary, uninspired, run-of-the-mill boys—are likely to take music, serious music, with a grain of salt and a sigh. To be compelled to sit at a piano, or stand under a violin, and do exercises, is a form of penance exacted from the youthful for the sin of being young. Too, it is humiliating, and sissy—and a God-awful waste of effort and sunshine.

And reading notes on a blackboard is a soulless pastime.

And concerts are in a category all by themselves.

Memorial Grammar School prided itself on being progressive. During the school year Miss Roth had periodically marched us out of its portals and escorted us on buses and streetcars to the Concert Hall. It was part of a program to endow us with culture, to metamorphize us into nine, nine-and-a-half, ten, ten-and-a-half, and eleven-year-old little ladies and gentlemen. It was all to enrich us spiritually.

Miss Roth would lock-step us into the auditorium, seat us, locate herself at a vantage point, and regard all forty-four of us, her pupils, with grim calm, benevolent malevolence. Miss Lewis and Miss Currier, Miss Merritt, Miss Dale, and Miss Georges would march in with 4B and 4A, 5B, 6B and 6A, and surround us. Mr. Eddy, our principal, would find a strategic spot and regard us savagely. I think he dreaded the concerts even more than we did. He *knew* that 5A would sooner or later do something to bring Memorial Grammar School into disrepute. And it always turned out that way.

In the beginning, before the music started, everything would be routine. The concert musicians would be on the stage monkeying with their instruments and making little dissonant noises. Occasionally one of them would hit a discord a little harder than usual and some schoolboy wit in the restless audience would start to applaud. Generally it was James.

A ripple of applause would widen and spread across the auditorium. It would get louder—decibels and decibels louder. Mr. Eddy would slowly rise to his feet and regard us warmly—except for his eyes. The applause would become thunderous. Mr. Eddy would give us a jolly smile —except for his eyes. He would lift his long arms just like the conductor and push down with the palms of his hands.

His lips would repeat and repeat, silently: *That's enough, children!*

Then, unless the ovation died away immediately, his lean face would darken and his fingers begin to twitch. He'd been a soldier in the Spanish-American War; possibly he was feeling for the trigger of an elusive Gatling gun.

As all things must, at last the uproar would peter out. The musicians would be careful not to make any more exceptional sounds. All over the Concert Hall there would be the hubbub of classes from a dozen schools from all over Cleveland—filing in, testing their seats, and craning their necks to see who and what was behind, above, beside, below. A great heterogeneous, homogenized mass of Italian-Americans, Hungarian-Americans, Anglo-Americans, Hispano-Americans, Scotch-Irish–Americans, Polish-Americans, Turko-Americans, Greek-Americans, Russo-Americans, Afro-Americans—Americans.

Then, after another quarter hour, just as we were about to perish with boredom, the conductor would suddenly appear and mount the podium. That was good for another roar of applause. Generally, this was the *critical moment*. All over the giant auditorium teachers would be throwing their weight around, policing and intimidating their charges.

The last concert before school let out saw James and Bob and me kicked out of the Concert Hall while twelve hundred students and Ignace Paderewski stood by. It was Paderewski that day instead of a conductor.

Everything happened in the critical moment.

Paderewski walked onto the stage and paused by the piano and regarded his audience. We gave him an ovation. Everyone applauded. But 5A always carried things to extremes.

Mr. Eddy got up and extended his arms and pushed down on the air and moved his lips. *That's enough, children!*

"Lookit 'at bastid," Bob said, nudging me. Bob sat on one side of me, James on the other.

"Lookit 'im," I said, nudging James.

"Which one?" James asked.

I turned to Bob.

"Which one?"

"Mister Eddy," Bob said to both of us. "He's tryin' ta fly . . ."

We gave Mr. Eddy an ovation and a new burst of enthusiasm enlivened the entire Concert Hall. For maybe twenty minutes we'd sat there, fidgeting, and looked at a grand piano on an otherwise empty stage. All twelve hundred of us had about reached our flash point.

Then George Hopper sat back in his seat and it closed on my toes. George sat directly in front of me. He got one of Bob's feet too.

"Hey!" I gasped. George was the school fat boy. "Hey, Fat," I whispered in great agony, "you're mashin' my toes. Get off, *quick!*"

"Jeez!" Bob said, scrunching down in his seat and trying to get his foot free.

George sat back, harder.

"Hey, dope!" I muttered. *"Get off!"* I'd tried to tell him in a forceful whisper. It came out a piercing yell.

George Hopper bounced his weight around. The twins and I had been annoying him while we waited for Mr. Paderewski. We'd been shooting rubber bands at the backs of George's ears. He was getting revenge.

He gave a big bounce. The auditorium was almost quiet.

"Holy Moses!" I screamed in the sudden silence. Mr. Paderewski had seated himself at the grand piano. "Fat, you're killin' me!"

"GET OFF!" Bob howled.

"Get off, *dope!*" James said, rising from his seat and coming to our aid.

George just sat, stubborn, and tried to make himself inconspicuous. Mr. Paderewski was no longer the center of attraction. We were.

I hit him on the ear. The left ear. Bob hit him at the same time on the right ear. James popped him on the left ear again. George shrieked and grabbed his ears and jumped up. Then, while I was frantically salvaging my toes, he turned, leaned over the seat, and hit me on top of the head. He hit Bob too—right on the Adam's apple. Bob made penetrating gurgling sounds and fell down between the seats with his eyes sticking out of his head. I heard clock chimes and church bells. George lowered the boom on me again. James lunged at him and fell down and

40

bumped his chin on the back of the seat in front. He got up with a howl and jumped up on his seat just in time to get pushed over backwards into the lap of On'wi Irene, the class snob. James bumped her in the face with the back of his head and when he scrambled up she didn't look the same.

(Once, in class, during a spelling bee, Miss Roth had asked Irene to spell *ennui*. Everyone else had failed. Irene didn't. She even went on to define it: *"On'wi,"* she enunciated, "is a feeling of listless weariness resulting from satiety." That's the kind of girl she was.)

Bob and I were on the floor. We hugged it. We were afraid to get up under George's fists. Bob was still making funny noises. And I'd suddenly realized the spot we were in. Mr. Eddy would be going into action any second now. The entire Concert Hall was in an uproar. The ennui was all over.

James was already corraled. Miss Roth had him by the hair. Irene was screaming bloody murder. Then somebody got hold of Bob by the feet and started dragging him out. It was Mr. Eddy. His face was horrible to behold.

Mr. Eddy should have let Bob crawl out by himself. As it was, all the golf balls and buckeyes Bob had in his pockets rolled out and started rumbling down the auditorium. Nine golf balls and six or eight buckeyes, and a couple of ball bearings, the entire wealth of the secret society, rolled from seat level to seat level.

41

Mr. Eddy got me by the hair and dragged me out too. Then he started all four of us up the aisle: the twins, me and George Hopper.

Miss Roth was taking Irene up the aisle ahead of us and holding a handkerchief to her nose. To Irene's nose.

"Leggo'a my hair," I begged, to no avail.

"You ain't allowed ta torture us," James said, keeping well ahead of Mr. Eddy and Bob and me, out of torture's reach. "You gotta tell our mothers an' fathers to!"

"*Woob!*" Bob wailed, walking on his tiptoes just as I was, trying to save some of his hair. "*Doob!* Jeez!" His Adam's apple still was on the blink.

"I didn' do a thing," George pleaded. "Not a thing! Them guys shot me with rubber bands—an' stuck feet in my seat—an' socked me on my ears. *I didn' do a thing!*"

"Liar!" James howled.

"*Silence!*" Mr. Eddy hissed. "*Modulate your voices! Silence, vipers—or I'll slay you, all—to the last one!*"

"*Woob!*" Bob wailed again.

Mr. Eddy took us out of the Concert Hall, all the way outside, and drove us from him, like moneychangers driven from the temple. He was in a great wrath.

Miss Roth came out; she'd left Irene somewhere inside. Mr. Eddy turned and gave Miss Roth a long, black stare.

"Gracious, Mister Eddy," she protested, coloring. "I couldn't do a thing. It happened so suddenly. They were sitting there like angels. I had just looked around. I

looked away—and when I looked back—there they were—
it was like an explosion!—really . . ."

"Miss Roth," Mr. Eddy said, inhaling and drawing
himself up to his full height of about nine feet (he was
standing on the steps above her), "you *teach* 5A, do you
not? Have you no *control* over them?"

"Really . . ." she protested.

He turned and stalked back into the Concert Hall.

"*Really!*" Miss Roth said again, indignant, and speaking
to no one. Then, under her breath, she muttered something about an old goat. Then she got a hold on herself—
and got back to us.

But she was so mad at Mr. Eddy that she couldn't rip
us up as good as usual. She said that we weren't to leave
the steps until the concert was over and the whole class
went back to school. She said that we, every one of us,
were going to stay in for forty-five minutes every day
for the rest of the semester! She said she'd think it over.
Maybe she'd have us expelled and sent to a reformatory!

She asked us if we weren't ashamed of making such a
spectacle of ourselves in front of so many other students?
And what would Mr. Paderewski think of Cleveland?

George Hopper began to whimper.

"Please, Miss Roth," he blubbered, "*I* didn' do a
thing. They were shootin' rubber bands at my ears . . ."

She stamped her foot.

"No wonder!" she said. "Your big dreadful head looks

like a taxicab with the doors open! You dreadful boy!"

George sat down on the marble steps and put his head in his arms.

"Oh, *my dear*," Miss Roth said, clasping her hands. "What have I done! What have I said! George, darling, you don't look *at all* like that!"

"Hell he don't!" James said.

"You wanta see my toes where he caught 'em in the seat?" I asked. "Betcha every one on both feet is busted!"

She got mad at us again.

"What on *earth* is wrong with you?" she asked, excited. "Why can't you be like *decent*, ordinary children? You do the *insanest* things. Don't you *ever* think first? You use bad language . . ."

"My Adam's apple . . ." Bob gasped, getting his speech back.

"*What?*"

"He got hit in the Adam's apple," I explained quickly. "He's just beginnin' to breathe now. That's why he's been makin' all those funny noises."

"I figured I was dyin'," Bob gasped.

"Miss Roth," James said, stepping into the breech, ignoring us and taking her hand. "You're not really mad at us, are you?" He said it in his most winning way.

"*Mad?*" Miss Roth said, a bit at a loss for words. "Only *dogs* become *mad*. I'm angry. I'm displeased. *I'm hurt!* I thought I could *trust* you boys. I thought . . ."

"Miss Roth," James said, still holding her hand, "you

c'n trust us! We like you th' best of all th' teachers, we do.
I've never seen you so pretty. You don't look more'n
thirty-five, all red an' everythin' . . ."

Miss Roth was speechless.

Just then Mr. Eddy stuck his head out of the bronze
doors and called to her: "Miss Roth . . ."

"Yes?" She turned.

He smiled apologetically. Then he smiled a bigger
smile. He'd seen the same thing James saw. We all had.
It was true. Being mad, that mad, became her; but probably it wasn't very good for her arteries.

"Don't you think you'd better come in?" Mr. Eddy
asked. "He's playing now. I wouldn't want *you* to miss
any of this."

She went. She passed him with her nose in the air.

But some time during the summer vacation he asked
her to marry him, and she said she would. But that's
neither here nor there.

We sat down on the steps beside George Hopper and
watched the traffic.

"Forty-five minutes after school every day!" I said.

"Flunked in music!" Bob said. "She'll sure flunk us!"

"Yeah," I said. "That means an extra class of music all
next year." It made me sick to think of it.

"Pop'll beat us up fer failin' a subject, less'n we c'n
talk him outa it," James mused.

"You sure did soft-soap *her!*" I said.

"Pop don't listen!" James said, depressed. "When he

45

gets a razor strop in his hand, he loses his hearin'."

"He looks like Abraham Lincoln without a beard, Mister Eddy does," George said. "Warts an' everythin'."

"We'll get notes ta our folks," Bob said.

"That means a beatin' all around," I said.

"I'm not ashamed of makin' a 'spectacle' of myself, are you?" James asked.

"No," I said.

"No," George said.

Bob shook his head.

"They're all just a buncha boobs!" James continued. "There goes a brand-new automobile. I hate music!"

"Lost all my golf balls," Bob said, feeling his pockets. "An' my lucky buckeye."

"I didn' wanta hear ole Paper Whiskey play th' piano anyhow," George said, looking up at one of the posters.

"Me, either!" I agreed.

"He's got lots of hair," James commented, looking at the picture.

"You sure fixed ole On'wi," George said.

"Didn' mean to, it was your fault, but I'm glad I did," James said.

"Miss Roth won't expel us an' send us to a reformatory," I said.

"She always says that," James said.

We sat there, thinking.

"There goes a *Stutz*," George said, pointing.

"What's the next one?" I asked.

"*Oakland*," Bob said.

"When're we gonna get 'at pup?" I asked.

"Soon's school's out, next week," James said.

"Right away," Bob confirmed.

"You gonna get a big dog, or a puppy?" George asked, interested.

"Pup," I said.

"Yeah," James agreed, "so's we c'n watch him grow up—an' train him ta like only us."

"He'll bite people we tell him to," Bob said.

"You gonna buy him? Or somebody give 'im ta ya?" George asked.

"Guess we'll have to pay money," I said. "If we was in South Dakota on th' Indian reservation we'd get him free. They got all kinds. Mary Heaven had seven dogs." I hadn't thought or spoken of her in quite a while.

"Who's she?" George asked.

"His girl. She's Indian. Sioux," Bob said.

"He's gonna marry her," James said.

"When?"

"Soon's I finish school," I said. "We used to go swimmin' together with all seven dogs. They'd scratch us up somethin' awful—like we'd been in a fight. We'd be swimmin' around an' they'd try ta crawl up on us. They'd scratch us all up with their toe nails."

"Where?"

"All over," I said. "Mostly on the shoulders, but all over. They were hound dogs an' their feet went way down in th' water."

"Din't you have on bathin' suits?" George smirked.

"Indians don' wear bathin' suits!" James said.

"Screwy!" Bob said.

But then all three of them looked at me, waiting.

"We was engaged to be married," I said. "The dogs crawled up on our shoulders. There wasn't nobody around. We got leeches all over us, suckin' our blood. We put salt on 'em to get 'em off. I put salt on hers an' she put salt on mine."

"Was she pretty?" George asked, chastened.

"*Gorgeous!*" I said, remembering her. She was. "She was gorgeous!"

"How old's she?"

I stopped and figured.

"Same's me, I guess," I said. "Nine. You shoulda seen th' mosquitoes. We had lumps all over."

"Once I got all scratched up," Bob said, remembering.

"He was learnin' ta ride a bike, a two-wheeler," James continued. "We was little kids. He got on th' bike an' got started; he'd kick the pedals every time they came around. Then he started down a hill. He couldn't get her stopped. His legs were too short fer brakin'. He just went faster an' faster until he got to th' bottom, then he skittered lickety-split across somebody's lawn and into a lot a' rose bushes . . ."

"A regular forest of 'em," Bob said, shaking his head. "Smack through th' middle."

"A man heard him yellin' an' came out of th' house," James said. "Bob'd stopped right in th' middle of th' thorns. They was so thick they held th' bike up, only he'd gone over the handlebars an' was lyin' in the stuff, makin' an awful racket.''

"They was all day gettin' me out," Bob added. "About a hour!"

"Anyhow," George insisted, "how're you guys gonna get money ta buy a puppy?"

"We got it figgered out . . ." James said, and didn't say anything more.

"Uhuh," I said cryptically.

Bob nodded.

"How?" George asked.

"None a' yer business!" we chorused.

"Nuts!" George said.

"After I got healed I had another accident," Bob said. "At church."

"Sunday school," James corrected. "He was still all over bandages an' adhesive tape. He was walkin' th' iron railin' out in front, showin' off—an' had about ten little girls watchin' him."

"Round railin'," Bob interrupted. "I slipped an' did th' splits, one leg on each side!"

We made a game of identifying all the makes of cars that drove by. *Model T. Ajax. Durant. Flint. Essex. Franklin.*

Then we sang. Patriotic songs. We sang *Mademoiselle from Armentières, parlez vous . . .*

Every now and then, from inside, would come a breath

of Mr. Paderewski's music. We moved farther down the steps so that the Hungarian Rhapsody wouldn't throw us off our own melody.

George sang soprano. James and I sang a mixture of soprano and alto. And Bob sang bass. He sounded as if he was singing with his head in a bucket. It was very melodious. He'd gotten that way from being hit in the Adam's apple.

We sang louder. *Mademoiselle from Armentières, parlez vous* . . .

No one could hear us. Behind us the doors were closed. The marble steps were as wide as the Concert Hall and we were right in the middle. We were removed from the sidewalk and street by the steps below us and the broad lawn and long walk.

We threw back our heads and sang until our tonsils vibrated. It was wonderful, being wicked so loud.

The Spring afternoon was warm and promising. The aroma of gasoline fumes from the cars in the street was exciting and soul-disturbing. Some of the drivers looked our way and smiled. Some of them waved.

"See that?" George interrupted.

"What?" we asked.

"A woman drivin'."

"She waved," Bob said.

"Looks funny t'see a woman drivin'," James said.

"My mother drives our car," I said. "It always looks funny!"

We began to laugh. We laughed until we rolled on the steps and got cramps in our sides and wet ourselves slightly.

"C'mon," George said, getting his breath. "Le's sing some more."

"Th' dirty part," Bob urged.

"Yeah," I agreed.

We sang.

> *Mademoiselle from Armentières, parlez vous?*
> *Mademoiselle from Armentières, parlez vous?*
> *Oh—the first three months all was well,*
> *Parlez vous?*
> *Oh—the second three months she began to swell,*
> *Parlez vous?*
> *Oh—the third three months she gave a . . .*
> *And a little Marine jumped out of . . .*
> *Hinky dinky, parlez vous?*

⋙ 7 ⋙

The Saturday Evening Post

W E DIDN'T get sent to the reformatory. We were kept in after school for three days, but then Miss Roth let us off. She always had somewhere to go, usually with Mr. Eddy. And she couldn't bear the punishment of punishing us. She forgot to give us notes to our parents. And she didn't flunk us. She passed us to 6B with the rest of the class; but she threatened that if we didn't work harder and get better marks in the Autumn, she'd keep us in 6B for the rest of our natural lives! Then she patted us on our heads and turned us loose for the Summer.

The day after school let out we took the twins' coaster wagon and hiked all the way to the city dump. It was a lot farther than we'd supposed. We didn't get there until late in the afternoon, but we found what we'd come for:

a hot-water heater. We three got hold of it, lifted it into the wagon, and started home.

We didn't get back until after 9:30 at night. We'd been gone since daybreak.

We stopped at my house. The twins were so weak from hunger that they couldn't go any farther. We had blisters on our feet that were three or four storeys deep.

My mother wasn't in.

"Where d'ya suppose she is?" James asked, sitting down on one of the kitchen chairs and collapsing over the table. Bob seated himself opposite James and lay his face against the smooth enamel tabletop. I tried it myself.

"Out lookin' fer me," I said feebly. I forced myself up and got some milk out of the icebox and a package of gingersnaps down from the cupboard. I was so hungry; I was giddy. James and Bob got three glasses. I said: "She's gonna kill me when she gets home!"

Bob giggled; he was so starved and exhausted that he was light-headed; his humor was strictly of the calamitous, gallows variety.

"We never been out this late before," James said.

"I'm supposed to be home and inside before dark," I said. "She's gonna kill me!"

Bob giggled again. The only thing that ever really amused Bob was himself in dire trouble or beaten up.

"Here . . ." James filled his glass with milk and shoved some gingersnaps at him. "Eat somethin'."

We each gulped a glass of milk. I filled up again out of

another quart bottle, all around. Then we took a breath, hooked our feet on the chair rungs, and began dunking gingersnaps.

"What're we gonna tell 'em?" I asked. We'd come in the house only after seeing that the lights were out and that my mother was absent; we had to figure out what we were going to say; we had to tell the same story—just in case our parents got together and checked up.

"Pop ain't gonna listen, anyhow," James said.

"Sure he will," I said. "He's a swell guy."

James didn't accept my view. He said: "He's gonna take us out to th' garage an' cut us in little pieces." He put a whole gingersnap in his mouth, shaking his head at the vision of himself cut in little pieces.

Bob had his nose in his glass of milk as James spoke. He giggled and inhaled about half the milk, then, stricken, blew it all over the kitchen, including James and me. He choked and gasped. It was quite a while before he got his breath. James cussed him out in telepathy. I wiped up most of the mess with a dish towel.

"Milk in yer hair," James observed.

"Yours, too," I said.

We wiped it out for one another.

"What'll we tell 'em when they get back?" I asked.

"Why not tell th' truth?" Bob asked in a foggy voice, suddenly sober. A trickle of milk ran out of his nose as his sinuses emptied themselves. I gave him the towel.

"Crazy?" I asked. "They find out we done it to make money for a pup, they'll *never* let us have it."

James nodded, serious. Bob shrugged; he smiled to himself.

"I'm gonna telephone home," James announced resolutely. "Maybe it'll be easier on us if they hear us, but can't get at us right off."

"Whatcha gonna say?" I asked.

"Search me," James said.

Bob and I ate gingersnaps and watched him while he got the number.

"Bell's ringin'," he told us, biting his lip.

We waited, apprehensive. Nothing happened.

"Nobody home?" Bob wanted to know.

James hung up.

"What're we gonna say?" he asked, desperate in a hopeless sort of way.

"Told ya so," I said. "They're out lookin'!"

"We been *kidnapped!*" James said, trying the idea out.

"Who by?" I asked.

"Criminals," Bob suggested, grinning into his milk.

"If yer gonna laugh, get away from 'at milk!" I warned.

The telephone rang.

We jumped.

Bob's mouth hung open and it was full of chewed-up gingersnaps.

"*You* answer," James whispered to me, suddenly cowardly. "It's *your* house."

"What you whisperin' for?" I whispered. "They can't hear us till we pick it up. *What'll I say?*"

"See what they say first," James suggested hoarsely, but gradually getting a hold on himself.

"Maybe it's a wrong number?" Bob said, giggling again. I had to giggle too. So did James. It was so awful it was funny. The phone wouldn't stop ringing.

It was the police.

They asked if the boys had shown up yet?

I said yes. The twins looked at each other, aghast.

"Is this the police station?" I asked, shaken to the roots.

"Yes, it's the police station," the telephone said. "You one of th' kids?"

"Yes, sir," I stammered.

"Where you been?"

"The dump," I said. "We walked."

"*Dump!*" the big voice at the other end said, repeating it to someone. "The li'l bastards been ta th' *dump*.

"All *three* of you?" the voice suddenly asked.

"Yes, sir," I said. James and Bob nodded. "Yes, sir. James an' Bob an' me."

"Yer folks there?"

"No, sir," I said, looking around. The twins looked behind them, then shook their heads. "Just us. We were eatin'. Gingersnaps an' milk. We didn't eat all day . . ."

"I wouldn't be in your shoes!" the voice said. "Not fer

all th' tea in China! Folks been all over town lookin' fer you!"

The twins went white. I felt kind of faint myself.

"Yes, sir," I said. "We're sorry, sir."

"We're goin' right home, Mister—" James said into the mouthpiece.

"Whozat?" the voice demanded.

"James an' Bob," I said.

"You tell 'em ta stay *right where they are!*" the voice said, full of authority. *"Right where they are!* Got that? *No more scatterin' around.* Tell 'em!"

"They heard you," I said. "They got their ear right here."

"What you do at th' dump?"

"We hadda get somethin'," I said.

"What?"

"A hot-water heater."

"A *what?*"

"Hot-water heater," I repeated, upset. "A hot-water heater, sir."

"Don' tell 'im why!" James whispered. I nodded.

"Why?" the voice demanded.

"T'make a helmet," I said. James got excited and shook his fist under my nose. I held my finger to my lips.

"Helmet?" the voice said. It turned aside from the phone. "They got a hot-water heater t'make a *helmet!*

"You're gonna need a helmet just as soon as yer folks get there!" the voice declared, booming into my ear. "You

kids stay right there. Right where you are! All three. Wait fer 'em, they'll be along directly. Hear?"

"They been there?" I asked weakly.

"They're probably out cruisin' around lookin' fer three kids," the voice said. "But they were here—an' they'll be here again."

"Good-bye," I said.

"They must be crazy!" the voice declared to someone else, and hung up.

I put the receiver back on the hook. We went back and sat down, numb.

We sat there twenty or thirty seconds before our appetites returned.

"I never knew it'd take so long out to th' dump," I said.

The twins were holding one of their silent conversations. Bob nodded. Then James nodded. Then both shook their heads in despair. They talked so fast I missed part of it.

"What?" I asked.

"He's gonna murder us, all right, all right!" James said.

"My mother always uses a rolled-up *Saturday Evening Post*," I said.

"Hah!" Bob snorted.

"Tha's nothin'!" James said. "Pop uses his razor strop —on our *bare* skin! We give him a safety razor on his birthday. He kept the strop anyway."

"I wish I was back in South Dakota," I said.

"With th' Indians," James said.

"Me, too!" Bob agreed.

"We could have all th' dogs we wanted without gettin' kilt gettin' 'em," I said.

"You could get married ta Mary Heaven," Bob said.

"Sure—" I said, dreaming. "An' you guys could come live with us an' be our kids . . ."

"Nuts!" Bob said. "You're younger'n us. Two years."

"Year'n a half," I protested. "What's th' difference?"

"Hell, yes," James said. "Who cares? Only we're *here!*"

"Maybe somethin'll happen," I said.

"Somethin'll happen, *certain!*" James said; he groaned.

Bob started laughing again.

We joined him.

The three of us laughed for two or three minutes, nonstop. Then, in extreme distress, we hurried into the bathroom.

"*W-w-w-w-h-h-h-h-i-i-i-i-u-u-u-u—!*" Bob exhaled, in relief.

"*Lord!*" said James.

"Funny, ain't it, how a guy works?" I said.

"Other day Mom caught Babe an' Myrtle havin' a contest out back a' th' garage," James said, "seein' who could shoot furtherest. Babe's a dirty little guy."

"Pop kilt him when he came home," Bob said.

"Not fer that," James explained. "Fer hittin' Myrtle. Him an' Mom talked it over that evenin'. They thought we was asleep. We was listenin' at th' door. Us two. Babe was asleep."

"Yeah?" I said. "What'd they say?" I was feeling much better now that the pressure was relieved.

"He ast her what happened," James continued. "She said she saw them out th' kitchen window. She said she didn' say anythin' because she didn' care ta make a 'issue' outa it. Then, all of a sudden, Babe started beatin' up on Myrtle. He loosened her front baby tooth. Mom yelled . . ."

"Why'd he beat her up?" I asked, buttoning up.

"I'm gonna get me a pair of them sailor pants some day," Bob said. "They look good."

"I'm always losin' buttons," I said. "An' they gotta be ironed inside-out so's the creases turn in at th' sides. What else'd your pop an' mom say?"

"She said she stopped it," James said. "Th' fight. She yelled out th' winda. Then she run out an' ast Babe wasn't he ashamed ta hit a girl littler'n he was! She promised him she'd have Pop fix him good! He did."

"An' then?"

"Well, they laughed a little bit." Buttoning up, we went back to the kitchen. "Then Pop ast who won? The fight? Mom said, why, Babe, of course. Poor little Myrtle. You know what I mean, Pop said. *William!* Mom said. Never mind that, Pop said, laughing some more, who did? Mom started laughin'. Myrtle, she said. That's why he hit her. I'll be damned! Pop said. He's no son of mine!

Sh-h-h—Mom said, you'll wake the boys. How'd she do
it? Pop asked. *William!* Mom said. Then they laughed
together, quiet like . . ."

"Then what?"

"Aw," James said, "then they started talkin' about th'
gas station, an' books, an' dresses, an' stuff."

"Ole folks don't get no fun outa bein' alive," Bob said.
"I hate ta see Mom an' Pop gettin' old."

"You guys got an awful nice father," I said. "He ain't
so old."

"He c'n be brutal," Bob said, which brought us back
to where we'd started.

"It's five minutes after ten o'clock," James said.
"Maybe we should've gone on home anyhow?"

"That policeman said not to," I reminded them. "You
better stay right here." I didn't want to meet my mother
alone.

"Why'd you tell 'im we went ta get a helmet?" James
demanded, reminded of the telephone conversation.

"Didn' matter . . ." I argued. "I didn' say what kind.
There's all kinds. War helmets. Football helmets. Fireman
helmets. American helmets. German helmets. Middle
Ages helmets. French helmets . . ."

"King Arthur helmets," Bob added. "Helmets with
spikes on top. Roman helmets . . ."

"Sure," I said. "They'd never guess we're gonna make
a deep-sea helmet."

James was pacified. But he cautioned us: "Don't anybody tell, huh? No matter how much they make us suffer."

Bob agreed. So did I.

"Not me!" I said firmly. "I'll never tell, not even if she wears out th' *Saturday Evening Post* on me!"

"What else we gotta get?" James asked. "Where's th' magazine?"

I got it out of my section of the cupboard—a popular mechanics magazine. We found the place.

"Air hose . . ." I pointed to the illustration and diagram. "An' pumps ta pump th' air."

"Weights ta sink us," James said.

"It shows here how automobile pumps c'n be hooked up," I pointed.

"Pop's got tire pumps at th' gas station," Bob said.

"Mister Daniels sells rubber hose in his drugstore," I said.

"Enema hose?" James said.

"Naw, beer hose—long hunks," Bob explained.

"Oh," James said, yawning.

"Mister Daniels don't know where I live, or my name," I said. "He know yours?"

The twins shook their heads.

All of us yawned.

"I guess we got air hose then," Bob said.

"What about th' winda in front a' our helmet?" James asked, finger on the picture.

"Cinch!" Bob said. He turned to me. "That mineral-water guy . . . He know where you live?"

I shook my head.

"Okay," said James. "What else we need?"

"Hunks a' lead ta hold us down."

"How about weights off'n scales in th' steel yard?" asked Bob. That settled that.

"Rope," said I.

"Clotheslines all over th' place," Bob observed.

"I guess we got everythin' jus' fer pickin' it up," James said. "Them ole turtles out in Mentor Marsh are jus' th' same as soup right now!"

"Hell, yes!" I said.

"Hell, yes!" Bob said.

"We're rich!" James said. "We'll be shippin' turtles all over th' place. T' Buffalo an' Akron an' Maryland, every damn place!"

"Hell, yes!" I said.

"Hell, yes!" Bob said.

"We'll have our pup in no time!" I said.

"What kind?" Bob asked. We all felt wonderful. We'd gotten to the point where we were selecting the pup.

"Any make's okay with me," James said.

"Jus' so's he's little in th' beginnin'," Bob said.

"Black an' white'd be nice," I said. The twins nodded agreement.

Then we yawned, all three, in unison.

And we paused in mid-yawn.

An automobile had come into the driveway.

"Our car," I said, recognizing the sound of the motor. "Look out th' window."

"What for?" asked James, looking trapped. "Even when

they shoot guys against a wall they cover their eyes first."

"Hide th' magazine," Bob said, pushing it back to me. I put it back with my stuff in the cupboard compartment. There were people coming up the back steps. I got back to my chair. We heard voices.

"Our folks musta met," James observed grimly.

Paralyzed, we watched the door open and Mrs. Scott and my mother walk in, Mr. Scott after them.

"Well, well!" Mr. Scott said, surveying us and smiling widely. "Here they are! Isn't this nice! I'm so glad you boys got home before your parents got worried. Well, well, well . . ."

The twins smiled a sickly sort of smile. My face muscles were all short-circuited.

"How dirty they are!" Mrs. Scott gasped.

"You remembered your address. Surprising!" my mother said. "You were gone quite long enough to forget where you lived."

"We been sittin' right here, waitin' fer you," James managed to say.

Bob and I nodded.

"We didn' have anythin' ta eat, all day, till just now," I added, trying to stir up a little sympathy. "Not a thing."

"No," Bob said.

"We had milk an' gingersnaps. I hope you didn' worry," I said to all of them, especially to my mother. "We got th' stuff outa th' ice box."

"Milk," Bob murmured.

Mrs. Scott had Babe in her arms, like a ventriloquist's dummy. He was snoring. She started to speak. Mr. Scott put out his hand and stopped her.

"Let me . . ." he said, turning again to us.

"I knew we could rely on you boys," he told us, still smiling; he'd been smiling since he entered. He brought his hands together with a loud clap, then rubbed the palms together. All three of us jumped as his hands met. "So you had milk? Good—good— we thought perhaps you'd had water. No-o-o-o, we weren't worried. We did ask the Fire Department and the police to drag the swimming hole—and look in the quarry. We thought you might be there. You see, we hadn't heard from you since breakfast— not since *before* breakfast!" He wasn't smiling any more.

"We took some toast along," James explained. "We et it on th' way."

"We never thought it'd take so long," I said.

"It was a mistake," Bob said respectfully.

"Oh, yes," Mr. Scott said, "I'd forgotten. You went to the dump, didn't you, eh? Nice little excursion! Have a good time? Find anything interesting? Meet any influential people? Speak up, boys! *Speak up!*"

I glanced at Bob. He gave me a return glance of extreme anguish.

"Well, nobody got anything to say?" Mr. Scott asked. "That's curious. You must've had a wonderful day. A *splendid* day! *We did* . . .

"Listen! When you didn't show up at lunch time, your

mothers thought they'd check up and see if . . .
Well . . ." He was still rubbing his hands together, palm
to palm, straight out, only faster now; I could almost see
the friction smoke curl up from between them.

"Well . . ." he repeated, searching for words, "we
won't go into that. You wouldn't be interested. *But we
had a grand time!*

"I closed the gas station at four o'clock. We met firemen. We watched them drag the swimming hole. We met
cops. We went to hospitals and morgues. We had two
flat tires. Oh, we made a glorious day of it!"

He stopped rubbing his hands together. He turned to
my mother and asked her: "What's the most sound-proof
room in the house? You don't mind, do you? I don't want
to wait on this any longer than I have to. It's after ten
and we don't want to disturb the neighbors."

Mr. Scott was very calm and businesslike. The twins
were tongue-tied and glassy eyed. I smiled at my mother.
She smiled back at me—only she held her mouth the
wrong way. She nodded to Mr. Scott.

"The bathroom, I suppose," she said. "Please, Mister
Scott, I'm not strong enough. Would you?"

He nodded gravely.

"Come, boys," he suggested.

"We just was," Bob said.

"Yeah," James mumbled.

"All three of us," I corroborated.

"Let's go again," Mr. Scott said, leading us.

My mother showed him the way. It was very dreamlike.
Mr. Scott locked the door.

"Take off your pants, boys," he said.

"Doncha wanta hear *our* side of th' story?" Bob asked.

"Not especially," Mr. Scott said. "You might as well
be first. Take off your pants."

Bob had a little trouble. His fingers wouldn't bend. Mr.
Scott helped him. James and I just leaned against the wall
beside the washbowl, and shook.

"Now," Mr. Scott said, seating himself, "just stand
between my legs. Now bend over. All the way—you
know how, we've been through this before . . ." He
bent Bob over one knee and closed his other leg over Bob's
feet, so that he couldn't kick. He lay his hand on Bob's
bare bottom and it shrank up to almost nothing—like a
snail when you poke it—Bob's bottom did.

"Well . . ." Mr. Scott said. He looked at James and
me. Then he went to work. The sound was terrific. It
almost peeled the tile off the walls. I didn't know anybody could yell so loud.

"Now, *you*," Mr. Scott said to James, releasing Bob.
"Take 'em off!"

Bob held onto his inflamed cheeks and made short little
jumps around the bathroom, grunting and blowing through
his teeth, face all twisted up until it wasn't even human.

"Yer humiliatin' us," James managed to say as his
father bent him over his knee and secured him.

"Is that what I'm doing?" Mr. Scott said—and began.

He was efficient as all get-out. James was even louder than Bob. Bob stopped jumping around and listened in awe.

"I guess the bathroom's the wrong place to do this," said Mr. Scott as he finished. "A man could lose his hearing this way."

James flung himself against the tile wall and flattened out against it in exquisite pain. He, too, held his incandescent cheeks and blew through his teeth.

"Please, sir," I begged, "we didn' mean anythin' wrong!"

"That's a good boy," Mr. Scott said. I had my pants around my knees. "Just step out of 'em now."

"*We didn' mean anythin' wrong, honest!*" I said.

"Of course not," Mr. Scott said. "But you deserve it, don't you?"

I was quaking so bad I couldn't speak.

"See?" Mr. Scott said. "Now listen to me—at least I'm honest. I don't tell you it hurts me more than it does you, do I?"

"No, sir," I said automatically, not understanding.

"Drop your pants, boy."

I dropped them.

He pulled me to him.

"My mother uses th' *Saturday Evening Post*, sir," I said.

"Does, eh?"

"Yes, sir," I was terrified of his hand; I'd just witnessed what it could do.

He bent me over and secured my legs against kicking. "I don't," he said. "I use a strap, or my hand. They're best. Not too easy. Not too severe. My father used to hold me out at arm's length and kick me for less than you boys've done today. A man can't appreciate his parents till he's past thirty. He had eleven sons . . ."

I remember seeing James and Bob with their fingers in their ears.

×××× *8* ××××

ℳoney

THAT was my introduction to the most active week
of my life.

The very next morning the little girl who lived just
down the block, Myrtle, Babe's girl, came over to our
house and yelled for me to come out.

I wasn't feeling so good. I'd had to kneel on my chair
at breakfast. And I wasn't allowed to go out. I was still
being punished. The twins hadn't shown up. I supposed
that they were being oppressed too.

Myrtle kept yelling until I had to go to the screen door
and tell her to go away. She had a big voice for a little
girl just barely five.

"Beat it!" I said. "I'm readin'."

"Ho," she said, "ho, ho . . ." She always started
that way. "Ho, ho, ain' ya on vacation?"

"I'm readin' just th' same!" I said, bitterly.

"Fairy stories?"

"No!" I said, impatient. "*Book of Knowledge.* I'm readin' how far it is to th' moon. *Beat it!*"

"Ho, ho," Myrtle said, "you got a spankin'."

"G'wan, beat it!" I warned.

"Be nice to her!" my mother admonished. "You know what I've always taught you: little girls are little mothers."

"Ho, ho," Myrtle said, trying to see in through the screening.

I threw my book down in disgust.

"You know what I've always told you about books!" my mother warned.

"Yes'm," I said, sighing. I recited: "Books are little people. Each one is a little person."

"Ho, ho," Myrtle chortled, pressing her nose to the screen.

"*Just th' same,*" I whispered, "*I betcha I know a little mother who's liable ta get busted over th' head with a little person!*"

"I heard that!" my mother said. "Aren't you ashamed?"

"Yes'm," I said.

"I wonder," my mother said.

"Sure I'm ashamed!" I said. "I'm ashamed of even bein' *alive!* What's th' use of even bein' *born?* A guy's kept prisoner in his own *house!* I already lost a whole mornin' outa my *vacation!* I might as well be *dead!*"

"Don't you dare raise your voice!" my mother said.

71

"I'm sorry," I said.

"Ho, ho," Myrtle said.

"Dear, I think you better go now," my mother suggested.

"Ho, ho, I come ta tell him somethin'," Myrtle said.

"What?" I asked.

"Ho, ho, ya want a puppy, huh? You'n Babe an' Bob an' Bud, huh? Ho, ho, huh?"

"Sure," I agreed, interested, "*sure!* Who's got puppies?"

"Somebody—ho, ho, somebody," Myrtle teased.

"C'mon in," I said. I opened the screen door and let her in. She went over and curtsied to my mother and sat on the divan, smoothing her dress.

"That's a pretty dress you got on," I said. "Yer mother make it?"

"Ho, ho," Myrtle said, nodding—pleased, but cautious.

"Who's got puppies?" I prompted.

"Ho, ho," she said. "Ya gonna hit me with a book?"

"*Never!*" I declared. "Not ever. Did I ever hit you with anythin'?"

"Uh-uh," she admitted. "Ho, ho, Babe did . . ."

"He's a bad boy," I said. "Who's got th' pups?"

"He didn' mean to," Myrtle said, frowning. "I love him. Ho, ho, he's *not* a bad boy!"

"I don't think so either," I agreed. "He's swell. Who's got them pups?"

My mother said something about my English and my perfidy.

72

"*Please* . . ." I begged.

Then I got back to Myrtle. I wanted to choke her. I smiled.

"Ho, ho," Myrtle said, smoothing her dress again. "Dora's gonna have puppies!"

"*Dora?* You *sure?*" We'd always wanted one of Dora's babies.

"She is!" Myrtle said, beginning to fidget. "Ho, ho. I gotta go now."

"How'd you find out?" I demanded.

Myrtle looked a little anxious.

"Be gentle. You're frightening her," my mother said.

I tried to hold myself down.

"How'd you hear, Myrtle?"

"Ho, ho, Bert an' Jimmy were talkin'."

"When'll they be born?"

"Pretty soon."

"*How soon?*"

"Pretty soon," Myrtle repeated, edging toward the door. "Ho, ho, I gotta go."

I let her out. Then I got back to my mother.

"Poor dear," she said, "you terrified her. And such a sweet little thing. You must be more gentle with little girls."

"May I go out now?" I begged. "I've *gotta* talk to somebody about them pups!"

"Do you think you've been punished enough?" my mother asked. "Do you realize the dreadful thing you did?"

"Yes'm," I said, trying to conceal my impatience. "Yes'm, I know I did somethin' very bad, which I'll *never* do again! Thank you for teaching me *right* from *wrong*. I'm gonna be a good boy for th' rest of my life an' make you proud of me."

"You can go," said my mother, interrupting me and turning away.

I tore out of the house. As I went I heard laughter. I didn't waste any thought on it.

I sprung James and Bob. I told Mrs. Scott they'd learned right from wrong. They agreed. She was a little dubious, but with me on the loose she couldn't very well keep them in.

At last we were outside.

We went over to the club house and lay down to talk. On our stomachs. Sitting was out of the question.

"Listen," I said, "Dora's gonna have pups!"

"Le's go," Bob said, starting to get up.

"Wait a minit!" James said. "We gotta have a conference first. What if Bert an' Jimmy're over there?"

"This is vacation," I said. "I guess we're th' only guys in th' whole world who been home all mornin'!"

"They won't be home," Bob agreed. "They'll be gone somewhere."

"Helmet okay?" James asked.

"Sure," I said. "Still in th' coaster wagon, under th' back porch."

"Le's go!" Bob insisted.

74

"Who'll we talk to about Dora?" James wanted to know.

"Ole man Coffee'll be workin'," I said. "Anyhow, we won't get anywhere talkin' ta *him*."

"Missus Coffee," Bob said.

We got up and started. Somehow we moved with greater purpose and more unity than we'd ever moved before. We were even in step. We understood one another a lot better. The twins felt it too.

"You sure can yell," James said.

"I guess all of us can," I said. "Your pop whaled th' daylights outa us."

"Sorta makes you a relation of ours," Bob said.

I didn't reply. I felt too full.

Just before we got to the Coffee house, I said: "Well, I figure a boy needs a man's influence once in a while. I didn' mind him spankin' me. Even if he is a lot harder'n a *Saturday Evening Post*."

>≋≋≪

We knocked. Mrs. Coffee didn't hear us the first time. We knocked again, louder. She shut off the vacuum cleaner and came to the door. She had a cloth on her hair.

"Hello?" she said.

"Good mornin', Missus Coffee," we said.

"The boys aren't here," Mrs. Coffee said. "I think they're down by the lake."

"Never mind," Bob said. "Thank you."

We felt much easier.

"We came to see you," James said.

"Me?"

"Yes'm," Bob nodded.

"About Dora," I said.

"What's that dog done now?" said Mrs. Coffee, looking displeased.

"Nothin'," Bob said.

"Nothin' at all," James confirmed.

Mrs. Coffee looked at me.

"She's gonna have pups, we heard," I said.

"Uhuh," the twins said.

Mrs. Coffee looked back at her silent vacuum cleaner, then looked at us again. She made up her mind. She un-latched the screen door and took the cloth off her hair.

"All right, maybe you better come in."

"Where's Dora?" asked James, inside. Bob and I looked around uneasily. We were deep in enemy territory.

"Out back, I suppose," Mrs. Coffee said. "Sit down, all of you. Have a piece of candy?"

We said no, thank you, but eased ourselves into chairs as Mrs. Coffee sat down, and we accepted the candy when she passed the cut-glass bowl around.

"What about Dora?" she asked.

"Is she really havin' babies?" I asked.

"Looks that way," Mrs. Coffee said, helping herself to a piece of candy. "And you want one?"

"Yes'm!" we said.

She smiled.

"If you don't mind," James said.

"We'd take good care of it," I said. "We always did want one of Dora's pups."

"All right," Mrs. Coffee said, "have another piece of candy."

"We can have a pup?" Bob asked.

"Yes, all right," she repeated, nodding.

"*No!*" we said, incredulous.

"You can have one," Mrs. Coffee said. "She's going to have plenty—if size means anything."

"A boy-dog?" I asked, remembering Mrs. Scott's terms.

"All right."

It was too wonderful to be true.

"Look, Missus Coffee," James began, steadying a bit, "Bert an' Jimmy don' like us very much."

"They just about hate us," I admitted.

"Yeah," Bob said.

"I know," Mrs. Coffee said, shaking her head. "They're going through that period."

We didn't tell her that they'd been going through that period for quite a while—about as far back as anyone could remember. The thought seemed to have saddened her.

"Then?" I asked, hesitant.

She passed around the candy.

"Never mind," she told us. "*I* told you you could have one, and you can. It's between you and me."

We got to our feet. But she wasn't done with us.

"Mind you, you can't just *have* the puppy," she said. "You've got to show me enough money for you to buy it a license. Otherwise, *no* puppy!"

"Yes'm!" I said.

"Don' worry," James said.

We'd figured we might even have to buy a pup. Now, just getting license money didn't seem like too much of a job.

"Two bucks," Bob said; he always had the facts at his fingertips.

"Exactly," Mrs. Coffee said, looking us over.

"How long we got?" I asked.

"I don't know," Mrs. Coffee said. "She's heavy. I guess she's due almost any time."

"Gotta work fast," Bob said, thoughtful.

"You've got a little while," Mrs. Coffee said, loosening the vacuum-cleaner cord. "You can't take the puppy the day he's born. They have to stay with their mother for a little bit."

That was better.

"Dora's out back," Mrs. Coffee said. Then she covered her hair and turned on the vacuum cleaner.

We went around back and looked at Dora. She was heavy, all right. She didn't even get up to bark at us; just lifted her head, wuffed once, and lay it down again. We hunkered down and patted her. We didn't talk. We were happy, but responsibility weighed heavily upon us.

After a while Bob said: "Pumps—an' air hose—an' weights—an' glass fer th' winda in front . . ."

"Rope," James added. "Then we gotta put everythin' together. Then we gotta get turtles, an' sell 'em." He didn't say it with boundless enthusiasm; it was going to be a lot of work.

"We better get started," I said. "First, we'll cut th' helmet off'n th' hot-water heater. An' cut a winda in front. I got a hacksaw an' blades; they was in our house when we moved in. Somebody forgot 'em. What you guys worryin' about?"

"I'm thinkin' about all th' stuff we gotta get," James said, "so soon . . ."

"What's th' diff?" I asked.

"One slip-up,—" James said, in dead earnest, giving Dora a last pat, "an' we get another beatin'. I d'know if my rear-end could stand another wallopin' very soon."

"You positive we'll sell plenty turtles?" Bob asked me.

"Hell, yes!" I enthused. "You saw th' magazine. We'll get letters from all over askin' us ta send turtles!"

"Maybe we'll open a factory," James mused, the factory before his eyes. "We'll can 'em. Till then we'll ship 'em around packed in ice. Maybe we'll make a lot of money."

"Le's get away from here before *they* come home," Bob suggested.

✖✖ *9* ✖✖

Crime Wave

W E DIDN'T exactly cast caution to the winds, but we took a lot of chances, considering the inflamed state of our rear ends.

We worked on the hot-water heater with the hacksaw, cutting a helmet-shaped hunk from one end, shaping the breastplate and shoulder slots, and chiseling a square window in the face. It was exhausting labor and murder on our hands.

During our rest periods we acquired the other stuff we needed.

We were most of the week swiping enough five-gallon demijohns to make a window for the helmet. We got them off a mineral-water truck. We spoiled one after another until we learned how to use the glass cutter we'd swiped out of the 5 & 10. At last we got a curved piece the right size and shape for the faceplate.

CRIME WAVE

We stuck the glass in place with marine glue and felt
we swiped out of an aquarium store. We plastered the
edges with tar dug out of a new street. We rigged a pump
out of tire pumps the twins swiped out of their pop's
filling station. And we got air hose by raiding the drugstore that specialized in hops, twenty-gallon earthenware
crocks, and rubber siphon hose. Those were the home-
brew years.

We got seventy feet of the red rubber hose in one roll—
and Mr. Daniels saw it go. He jumped across the phar-
macy counter and chased us almost two blocks. But our
wind was better than his.

Our chest and back weights were plundered from the
scales in the steel yard down by the railroad tracks on the
way to Collinwood High—after dark. The twins pulled
the job. They took Babe along and swore him to secrecy.
Mr. and Mrs. Scott had gone to a movie at the Commodore
Theatre and left the boys in bed. The boys got up and
went after the weights; they got back only seconds before
their parents did. It was close.

After that Babe got in the act. He went over to Myrtle's
house and stole her mother's clothesline. Myrtle helped.
She was his lookout.

Then we had everything. All we had to do was put it
together. We didn't waste any time.

But we did go over to the Coffee place three or four
times a day to see how Dora was coming along. She got
heavier and heavier and moved from out back to in front

of the house, the front porch, where she could watch traffic go by.

Bert and Jimmy were savage when they learned that we'd been promised a pup. They told us, right in front of their mother, that we'd never get it! Mrs. Coffee didn't say anything. She just nodded to us to go ahead and earn enough for a dog license; she'd see to it that we got the pup.

We were sorry for her. We knew for certain that her boys were no good. And we'd heard—I don't know how, but I think Myrtle told us—that Mr. Coffee sometimes hit her.

><><

Then, a few days later, we were over there again, all four of us—James, Bob, Babe, and me—looking at Dora and wondering how long she was going to take, when Bert and Jimmy came out of the house, yelled at us, and kicked Dora off the front porch.

That started one hell of a fight. The twins were eleven. I'd been nine in February. The Coffee kids were thirteen and fourteen—big bruisers.

"Yay!" Bob howled, furious, as Dora got kicked.
Dora yelped.
"*Bastids!*" James howled.
"Get 'em!" I howled. Already we were on our way.
Babe stayed out of it.
Jimmy and Bert came down the steps and stood in front

of the house—and let us come. I was never so beat up in all my life, before or since. Our fingers and hands were so tender and puffed up from working with the hacksaw that it hurt us even to make fists.

"Hah!" Bert said as I rushed in. Then I was lying in a prickly hedge. I painfully unhooked myself, got up, and rushed back into the fray.

"Hah!" Bert said again. I got out of the hedge again. He kept saying *Hah!* and I kept getting out of the hedge. Each time I went into the hedge I got scratched in forty-seven thousand different places. I was knocked down in another direction for a change and it felt comparatively good.

I got up, got knocked down again, and got stepped on by one of the twins on his way into the thorns. The other one fell on top of me. But we didn't stay on the ground, or in the hedges—that was impossible—or any place. We kept harrying Bert and Jimmy. If the fight had lasted a little longer we might have dragged them down.

But Mr. Coffee came home. He was a policeman in the amusement park. He caught us from behind. Babe shrieked some sort of warning. He'd been dancing around out on the sidewalk, screaming encouragement, but we didn't understand. We were too busy.

A big hand took hold of the back of my head and pressed me forward—right into Bert. He popped me smack on the nose—I couldn't duck—and handed me to Jimmy. He hit me on the nose—twice. Then I fell over one of the twins and landed on my knees on the brick walk. Then the other twin fell over me; Bob, I think it was. Then there was a lot of mean laughter and I got kicked on my backside and told to get off their property!

I couldn't see—my nose made my eyes water—but I got away before I was kicked again. The twins came with me· We'd been annihilated.

We retreated across the street to where Babe was and stood there a while, looking over at the Coffees.

Mr. Coffee laughed and went into the house. My nose was dripping; I was blood all down the front of my shirt; and my front pocket was gone, torn off. That meant the *Saturday Evening Post* when I got home. I hurt all over.

At last my eyes stopped watering long enough so that I could see Mrs. Coffee inside their screen door. She had her hand to her heart and looked terribly sad. She'd seen everything.

"Please, Missus Coffee," Bob yelled across to her, "don't be mad with us. We won't do it again. You'll let us have the pup, won't you?"

It was the longest speech I ever heard him make. It wouldn't surprise me if it was the longest speech he ever made. She shook her head that she wasn't angry with us. I suppose that she was more upset about the way we looked than at our fighting her boys.

Bert and Jimmy were yelling at us to come back on their property and get beat up some more.

CRIME WAVE

"G'wan," I yelled, "if it wasn' fer yer poor mother standin' there, we'd smash ya one—ya bums!"

Mr. Coffee came to the window and told his boys to shut up and get in the house, right away. Dora sneaked around back and vanished. Then I saw what had happened to the twins—and I knew what I must look like. It was downright tragic.

"Yah, ya dirty bums!" James yelled after them. "Kickin' a poor li'l ole pregnant dog . . ."

"Shut up!" Bob said, pushing him. "Don't talk filthy!"

James pushed back. I guess we were pretty wrought up. James finished what he'd been about to yell when Bob interrupted. James threatened: "Ya ever do 'at again— ya hurt our pup afore he's born—an' ya'll see! Ya dirty bums!"

"Ole stink pots!" Babe shrilled. "Poops!"

"Keep quiet, you!" the twins warned.

The screen door flew wide as the Coffees burst from inside and started for us. But their old man's voice summoned them back; and he meant it. We stood there, opposite the house, long enough to show them we weren't afraid, then started home.

We broke up about a block away. Bob, James, and I each had a little crying to do—and we couldn't hold it much longer. And we preferred not to do it in front of one another.

I picked an alley.

85

My knees were all chewed up from falling on the bricks, I was scratches all over, and my nose was a nightmare. I sat down behind a garage and stuck my nose between my knees and let pain and grief and mortification gradually overcome me.

><><><><

We finished the diving rig the next day, put it in the coaster wagon, and hauled it two miles out beyond Euclid Beach Park to an irrigation ditch, or whatever it was. I got in the icy artesian water and Bob helped lower the helmet over me and James pumped. It worked swell. The water wasn't more than three and a half feet deep. I had to sit down to get the helmet wet, but it showed us that the thing worked. That made us feel better. Now all we had to do was make money.

Then, the following day, Dora came across. Myrtle brought us the news. We were in my backyard, putting a few finishing touches to our creation. We were splitting a length of garden hose and fitting it to the lower edge of the helmet; the ragged edge of the metal cut our shoulders unless it was covered.

"Ho," Myrtle said, coming through the fence, "ho, ho."

"Hi," Babe said.

"Whatcha doin'?" she asked.

"Fixin' up our drownin' suit," Babe said, being witty. "We're gonna drown oursel's."

"Shut up!" James said.

"Ho, ho—who?" Myrtle asked. "Me?"

"Him," Bob said, giving Babe a little kick.

"I'll tell Pop!" Babe warned, jumping out of harm's way.

"Y'do, an' we'll kick ya outa th' secret society!" James threatened.

"I gotta pertect myself," Babe argued.

"Grow up," Bob suggested, holding the end of the hose while I fastened it.

"When I do, I'm gonna beat all of ya up!" Babe said, scowling.

"Fat chance," James said. "Get outa my way."

"Go kiss Myrtle," I said.

"Ho, ho," Myrtle said, grinning, "sure."

Babe turned and ran. Myrtle started after him. She stopped for a moment and looked back at us.

"Hey," she said, "ho, ho."

"Ho, ho, yerself," James said, struggling to get the helmet into the coaster wagon, and failing. "Beat it. We d'want any kids around here. We got important business."

Myrtle stuck out her tongue.

"A'right," she said, pushing up her nose and pulling her lower eyelids down, using both hands. "Then I won' tell ya!"

"What?" I asked. "He didn't mean anythin'."

"No!" she said, looking like Quasimodo.

"We'll help catch Babe if you tell," I bargained, sensing something of great import.

"Ho, ho," she nodded, agreeing. "We alla time kiss in our closet, at my house. I wanta kiss where somebody c'n see."

"Yeah, yeah," I said. "What ya gonna tell us?"

"Cross yer heart ya'll catch 'im fer me?"

We crossed our hearts.

"Dora's got pups!"

10

*D*rat!

W E HADN'T been around the Coffee place
since the battle. But now we forgot danger.

We slowed a little and moved en bloc as we went up
the front walk and knocked on the door—no vanguard
and no laggards.

Mrs. Coffee answered. She was the only one at home.

"Come in," she smiled. "Through the house. Dora's in
the kitchen, under the stove."

The pups were terrific. Dora hadn't been very particular
when she went looking for a husband. But, for that matter,
none of the dogs in her family had been very particular,
not for generations and generations. The pups were
breathtaking. There were ten. They were tiny and wriggly
and their eyes were closed. They just squeaked and wig-
gled around against Dora's tummy. And one of them was
ours. That was the important thing. They were too small
to touch.

"Well?" Mrs. Coffee asked. "What do you think?"

We three were on our knees beside the box. Bob was first to come to his wits.

"Missus Coffee," he said, "they're handsome! Want to buy a turtle?"

"*What?*"

I explained. Like Bob, I'd suddenly remembered that we had to show enough money to buy our pup a license.

"It's like this," I said. "We're in th' turtle business. We get turtles for people who want ta eat 'em."

"That's th' way we're makin' enough money fer a dog tag," James explained. "D'you want ta buy a turtle ta make soup? We'll let *you* have one cheap."

"Ugh!" Mrs. Coffee said. "*Eat* a *turtle?* Who ever heard of such a thing!"

"They're good!" James said, taken aback by her attitude. "They're *delicious*. It said so in a magazine. People pay a lot of money!"

"Heavens!" Mrs. Coffee said. "Have you sold any yet?"

"No, ma'm," I admitted. The twins were down with the puppies again. "But we're startin' t'day. *Right now.* We're gonna go to every house an' get orders."

"Not in this neighborhood, you're not!" Mrs. Coffee said. "This is a good, God-fearing, Christian neighborhood. You'll sell no turtles here!"

We thought it over a minute. The twins talked it over between themselves without looking at each other or saying a word. We hadn't considered that anybody might not want to buy a turtle. We still didn't believe it, but the thought was unnerving.

"Was *that* the way you were going to earn money to buy a dog tag?"

The twins looked at me. It'd been my idea. I'd found the mechanics magazine. I answered: "Yes'm . . ."

"You got the turtles?"

"No'm," I said, "they're in th' swamp."

"Where? What swamp?"

"Mentor Marsh."

"Where's that?"

"About twen'y-five miles from here," James said.

"*Twenty-five miles!*"

"Yes'm," I said.

"Child," Mrs. Coffee said, "if you get any 'orders,' and if you catch any, how're you going to bring them in?"

"We'll catch 'em all right, all right!" I said, staring Bob and James down. "We've got a divin' outfit. We'll hitch rides out there an' back. We'll bring back gunny sacks fulla turtles!"

"In whose automobile?" Mrs. Coffee asked.

It was a discouraging conversation. Mrs. Coffee told us that it'd be a while before the puppies could leave their mother. She said that if we worked hard and didn't think up any more foolishness, we'd most likely have the money in time. She said that we could get jobs selling newspapers, or mowing lawns, or something, and make enough.

Out on the street again, I gave the twins a talk. I told them to take one side of the street and I'd take the other. We'd show Mrs. Coffee. We'd sell a *ton* of turtles!

We met at the corner. I'd rung every bell, and they'd covered their side. We hadn't sold any turtles.

I asked them: "What'd they say?"

Bob shook his head. James answered: "One ole guy ast was we crazy?"

"Maybe this *is* th' wrong neighborhood," I said, "jus' like she said. Maybe . . ."

"Look," James said, sticking out his jaw at me, "I been thinkin'. We both been thinkin'. How're we gonna get all 'at divin' stuff out to th' marsh?"

That had struck me too—the third doorbell I rang. It weighed eighty or ninety pounds, pump and all, maybe more.

"On th' coaster wagon," I said bravely. "We'll pull it out. *We'll walk!*"

"I got a notion ta bust ya right on th' nose!" Bob said, addressing me.

"Yeah!" James said grimly. "Fer all th' stuff we swiped, we could be put in Sing Sing. 'At mineral-water guy's lookin' fer us. We dassn't go in a ten-cent store any more, jus' in case we get recognized . . ."

"There's hardly *any* place we c'n go any more!" Bob said, working himself up.

"Lissen," James went on, eyes narrowing, hands clos-

ing, "when Pop says fer us t'go to th' corner drugstore
an' get him a cigar, we gotta go eleven blocks, *each way*.
We don' dare let Mister Daniels see us. We gotta go all
th' way down by the Commodore Theatre. An' Pop buys
his cigars one at a time!"

"*Twen'y-two blocks, runnin', every evenin'!*" Bob gritted,
making fists.

"An' then he asks why we been so slow!" James said.

The twins had reached their flash point. I got set.

But just then the Coffee boys showed up way down the
street. We decided that we'd better be moving along.

><><

We went over to my house and examined the diving
outfit. It looked complicated and wonderful; it made us
proud.

James pumped the pump and air hissed into the helmet.
It was on its side.

Bob got down and stuck his head into it. It was too
heavy to pick up.

James and I took turns pumping for the next ten minutes while Bob lay there, breathing.

Then James took a turn at sticking his head in the
helmet. Then I had my turn. Then, refreshed, we went
over to the empty lot next to the Scott house and sat in
the big hole we used for a clubhouse. We sat there and
meditated for a while. I broke the silence.

"Gosh," I said, "it works swell. We should oughta be able ta make money with it."

Bob nodded, preoccupied. James thought it over.

"Yeah," he said at last, "maybe if we were out by th' lake some time, maybe somebody would drown an' you could go down in it an' bring up th' body an' get us a reward."

"Who?" Bob asked. "*Me?*"

"*Him,*" James said. "He got us inta this fix!"

Then we were silent a while. I thought of what it would be like to find a dead corpse in the mud on the bottom of a lake, and touch it. I decided that the twins must be pretty mad at me.

After a little bit we crawled out of the hole and went over to the amusement park at Euclid Beach. We stopped by the penny arcade and the twins stood lookout while I went in and looked for pennies on the floor. I didn't find any, but I shook some peanuts out of one of the crane machines. And I saw the last few seconds of a picture in a penny stereopticon; someone hadn't gotten his full penny's worth. A lovely woman in a chemise combed her long hair in jerks.

On the way out, I heard a bat squeaking behind the gypsy fortune-telling machine. I forced myself between the machines and found the bat clinging to a niche in the brick wall, thinly muttering in his upside-down sleep. I grabbed him. He bit me. I turned loose, jostling the mechanical gypsy lady in her glass seance chamber. There wasn't time to make another try after the bat. The twins were giving the secret alarm: Bob howling like a wolf and James screeching like a screech owl. The penny-arcade man was coming.

Frantically I backed out of the crevice. The vibrating gypsy lady nodded at me just as I got free. The mechanism whirred and spat out a slip of pasteboard, then another, then another. It kept on spitting them out. I couldn't wait. I took the first three and ran.

Out of danger, we split up the peanuts and the fortunes. James read aloud:

"You will marry your present lover and be blissfully happy. Control your temper and think beautiful thoughts."

James spat through his front teeth and shook his head in disgust.

Bob read his:

"Do not worry. He adores you. You will bear him three daughters. You should wear red. Watch your weight!"

Mine read:

"Do not rely on artificial beauty aids. He will want you for yourself alone. Develop charm and poise."

We wandered on down to the pier that stuck out into Lake Erie. People were sitting along the edges, fishing. We went out to the end along one side, and back on the other. There wasn't much being caught. But something very significant happened out near the end of the pier. While we watched, one old lady got her line fouled under-water—tangled in the pilings. A man came over and helped her. But the line broke when they tried to pull it free.

"Drat!" the old lady said. She started gathering up her things and winding up the remainder of her line. "Drat!" she said again, "them pilings must be like pincushions! That's the third line I've lost in a week. This last one was the best. It had a catgut leader!"

"I lost a hook an' sinker this mornin'," the man said. "There must be a fortune in hooks an' sinkers down there."

"Pardon me, lady," Bob said. "How much you figure you lost?"

"In money?" she asked, looking at him.

"Yes'm," James answered. Bob had about shot his bolt as far as holding a conversation was concerned. "Yes'm."

"Right now—or all week?"

"Right now."

"About fifteen cents! Them hooks cost two cents each. The sinkers the same. That's ten. The catgut leader cost five cents. I'm not countin' the line. *Drat!*"

"Lady," James said, "if somebody, maybe a deep-sea diver, was ta salvage what you lost—what'd it be worth t'you?"

The old lady got mad.

"Go away, you kids!" she said loudly, waving her hands. "I got trouble enough without fresh kids!"

"He wasn' bein' fresh," Bob said.

DRAT!

"*Drat!*" the woman said. She got her stuff together and left the pier.

The man who'd helped break her line had gone back to his pole.

"Mister," I said, "what d'you think? If somebody, like us, was ta get all th' hooks an' sinkers an' bring 'em up here, on th' pier, d'you think people'd buy 'em?"

"Why not?" he asked. "Why not—at half price? All that weren't rusted into ruination. The sinkers wouldn't be rusted. Only there's no way."

I looked at the water. The pilings disappeared way down deep in it. We'd tested the diving outfit in a ditch. I'd had to squat down in the deepest spot so that the water would close over me. Nobody'd have to squat down there. It gave me the jim-jams just to think of it.

Bob and James talked over the salvage business, silently, all the way home. I didn't miss anything.

"We haven't even got a boat," I argued as they got to the part where I was to go down first. "We'll get pinched, sure, if we try divin' off'n th' pier!"

The twins didn't say anything.

"Look," I said. "I'll betcha Mister Coffee'd be out there an' arrest us in two minutes! Nobody's allowed ta swim off'n th' pier."

"Ya wouldn' be *swimmin'*," Bob observed.

"No," James agreed, "you'd be *walkin'* around."

"On th' bottom a' th' lake," Bob added.

"Why me?" I asked.

"You're th' guy wanted ta build a divin' outfit," James said. The logic was all on their side.

"Anyhow," I insisted, "we haven' got a boat, an' we can't work from th' pier!"

"We'll get one," James said, undaunted. "We've swiped everythin' else."

Bob nodded.

>⋙⋘<

Myrtle was waiting for us at my house. She had news.

"Say," she said, excited, "you tol' me you were gonna get one of th' puppies?"

We agreed, positive.

"Well, yer not!" Myrtle said, swallowing. "Know what? They're gonna kill all of 'em, Bert an' Jimmy are. Their daddy said to. He said th' puppies weren't any good!"

We ran down the street, frantic.

Bob was the best runner. After two blocks he was an entire block ahead of James and me. He tore into the driveway beside the Coffee house and disappeared in the backyard. By the time we got to the front gate, he was coming out again. He had a box in his arms, Dora's bed, and Dora was running beside him, worried. He had all her pups in the box.

James asked: "Missus Coffee didn' say not ta take 'em, huh?"

"Uh-uh," Bob gasped, still running, "she said to."

James jerked a paling off somebody's picket fence and I got another, just in case the Coffee boys showed up and tried to jump us and get the pups back.

We got them over to the twins' house okay. We put the box in the garage and Dora got into it and began nursing her babies. James and I settled down to figuring out which belonged to whom? We had ten pups to divide among the three of us—four, counting Babe. There was enough for everybody. We were rich!

Bob went into the house and came back with a pint of milk and a package of sausage for Dora. He took a long look at Dora's family while she ate.

"Hey," he said, thoughtful, "what if they want 'em back?"

"They're ours!" I declared.

"She give 'em ta ya, didn' she?" James asked, sticking out his under lip.

"Yeah," I said, understanding Bob, *but what if they do? Bert an' Jimmy?* I bet they come over an' try'n get 'em back—so's they c'n kill 'em!"

James stood up from beside Dora's bed. He still had his fence picket. He brandished it. Dora growled.

"Let 'em come an' try," James said.

"Put th' stick down. Dora's gettin' worried!" Bob said.

"Listen, you guys," I said, trying to be constructive. "We'll take our divin' outfit over t'morra an' make enough money fer dog licenses—all ten. I guess if we do that, an' get tags an' a paper showin' we paid, that'll make th' pups ours, *legal!*"

James agreed. He got enthusiastic.

Bob counted the pups again. Ten. Two dollars each for the boys; more for the girls.

"Fishhooks?" he said. "Lord, we'll have ta hold up a bank!"

"Maybe somebody will drown," James said hopefully, nodding toward me, "an' him get us th' reward."

>≋≋≋≪

Mrs. Scott called my mother and asked if I could stay with the twins for supper. She said she'd send me home before it got too dark.

Supper wasn't altogether a success. That is, it wasn't restful. Mr. Scott kept complaining about what this world was coming to. Sneak thieves had stolen four brand-new tire pumps out of the gas station.

Then, when supper was over, Mrs. Scott discovered that the cream to put over the peaches for dessert was missing. She was still in the kitchen, looking in the icebox and thinking out loud, when James said:

"Mom, we got our pup from Missus Coffee. The one she promised. We didn' know it was cream. Dora drank it."

"Land!" Mrs. Scott said from the kitchen. "Where's the sausage for your father's lunch tomorrow?"

Mr. Scott had started to eat his peaches without cream.

Now he paused. He put down his spoon. He looked at the twins. Babe snickered. Bob and James talked it over without saying anything. Bob shrugged and put some peaches in his mouth. James had to explain.

"It's like this . . ." he began, looking at his plate and pushing the peaches around, searching for words. "Bert an' Jimmy were gonna kill all th' pups an' so we went an' got 'em an' brought 'em home. Dora's gotta eat if she's gonna take good care of her babies, don' she? We had ta show Dora we loved her, didn' we?"

"Where's the sausage?" Mr. Scott asked quietly.

"They ain't weaned yet," Bob said.

"I wasn' around! I didn' have nuthin' t'do with ut!" Babe said earnestly. "I wasn' anywhere's around, honest!"

"Where'd the sausage go?" Mr. Scott asked.

Mrs. Scott came to the door of the dining room.

"William," she said to Mr. Scott, "be patient. Control yourself. We got company. I can buy more in the morning. I can make cheese sandwiches."

Mr. Scott didn't look away from the twins. He demanded: *"Where's my lunch sausage?"*

"Dora et it," James said.

"I give it ta her," Bob said.

"I didn' have nuthin' ta do with ut! Not a thing!" Babe said in panic.

"We got ten pups," I said, smiling warmly, "out in th' garage."

Mrs. Scott supported herself against the door frame.

Mr. Scott smiled. He put down his napkin.

"I was over ta Myrtle's house," Babe insisted, pale. *"I didn' have nuthin' t'do with ut!"*

"Sonny," Mrs. Scott said to me, "you better go home now. Your mother'll be worrying. It's dark out."

Just then someone rang the doorbell. Mr. Scott turned on the porch light and answered it. Bert and Jimmy Coffee pointed at us and said that we'd stolen their dog and all her pups! Mr. Scott looked at us and said that he didn't doubt it.

"No! It ain't true!" Bob yelled.

"No, sirree," James yelled. "She give 'em ta us on account they was gonna murder 'em. Golly, Pop!"

"We didn' steal a one!" I said. I appealed to Mrs. Scott: "You wouldn' want 'em killed, would you?"

She shook her head that she wouldn't. Mr. Scott wasn't listening.

"Come on," he told the Coffees. "I think I know where they are."

Babe started to scream.

James and Bob rushed toward the kitchen door and the back way.

"No, you don't!" Mr. Scott bellowed. "NO, YOU DON'T! Go to your room. *Right now!"*

Babe howled louder.

"G'wan, *run!*" Bob said, pushing me. "Save 'em!"

"*Run*," James said, "you don' have ta obey—you ain't one of th' fambly. *G'wan!"*

DRAT!

I went.

I ran out the back door and fell down the steps. I fell again over the garbage can at the bottom. I reached the garage and Dora's box and got hold of two pups. Dora got nervous at my suddenness and she nipped me on the ear. As I started out with the pups I ran into Mr. Scott and fell down again. The Coffees grabbed at me, but I was gone. I ran out onto the driveway and burst through the rosebushes and hedge. I kept going until I found our club house in the field. There I halted in the darkness. No one followed. I'd escaped.

I sat down in the hole and cried a little, a pup in each hand. I dried my eyes with one of them. My knees were all skinned again. And so was an elbow, from my fall over the garbage can. And going through the rosebushes hadn't done me any good. The pups whimpered and wriggled. I could feel their tiny hearts beat against my fingertips.

I hid there about an hour. I put the puppies inside my shirt, next to my skin, so they'd think I was Dora and not whimper. It worked.

When I was positive that the coast was clear, I crawled up out of the club house and went back to the twins' house. Their room was in back. I found the window. It was dark, but I could hear sobbing inside.

"*Hey,*" I whispered, putting my face to the screen. "Hey, you guys. We still got two pups. I saved 'em. What happened?"

Then Dora came to the window and sniffed me and whined. She'd scented her pups. The boys had her inside with them. Then I knew that something was wrong.

Bob opened the screen and I handed him Dora's babies. He gave them to James and helped me climb in. He'd been crying and so had James.

"What's th' matter?" I whispered. "Get a beatin'? Look, I fell down an' skinned both my knees an' my elbow."

The twins were in their pajamas. Bob had made a bed for Dora out of their two pillows and we watched her nuzzle the two pups and lick them.

"Naw," James said, wiping his tears on his pajama sleeve, "Pop didn' whip us. He's sorry. He's awful sorry. You don' have ta whisper. He won't do anythin'."

"What happened?" I asked. "I been hidin' in th' club-house. Where's Babe?"

"Pups're all dead," Bob sniffled.

"They're alive!" I said, dropping down beside Dora and touching one. "I took good care of 'em!"

"Th' rest . . ." James said. "After Pop gave 'em back, Bert an' Jimmy got a bucket of water an' drowned all eight out in front a' our house. Right in front a' Dora! When they was dead, they rang th' doorbell again. Pop opened th' door an' Bert an' Jimmy were gone, but th' bucket with th' pups floatin' around was there. Dora was too—all distracted. Pop buried all eight in th' garden. Babe's been havin' hysterics ever since. They got him out in th' front room."

"Uhuh," Bob said, "an' Bert yelled they was gonna kill these two—soon's they found 'em."

We took turns patting Dora and stroking her and telling her not to feel so bad. All four of us cried a little bit. Then, after we decided we'd hold a proper funeral in the morning, I decided that I'd better be getting along home.

I went out through the front of the house. Mr. and Mrs. Scott were sitting there. Mr. Scott was holding Babe in his lap; Babe had fallen asleep, but his face was swollen from crying. Mrs. Scott said Lord, my mother'd called about umpteen times, worrying why hadn't I come home. Mrs. Scott went out to the telephone in the hall and I apologized to Mr. Scott for being so disobedient. He shook his head.

"Never mind, son," he said. "I'm the one who's sorry. Damn the sausage! What happened to the pups you got?"

"I saved them, sir," I said, "two. They, James an' Bob, got both of 'em back there in their room. Dora's takin' care of 'em. I got in through th' window."

He nodded. Mrs. Scott came back into the room.

"You're to run home, right away!" she said. "I told her there'd been a little tragedy over here. I think everything's fixed up, but you better run all the way."

Randolph

I GOT out of the house just as soon as my mother decided that I'd had enough breakfast. It was hard to eat. I kept thinking the funeral might be over before I got there.

When I arrived at the twins' house they were in the backyard.

"We been waitin' on you," James said soberly. Babe looked sort of moist; he pointed to the grave. The pups had been buried at the edge of the garden, close under the rosebushes. The boys had smoothed out the surface and put a border of pebbles around the edges. Bob was kneeling beside the grave and pulling the petals off some roses and strewing them over the plot.

"C'mon, help me," James said, gathering roses. "We gotta get enough t'cover th' grave."

We gathered every rose in the garden. Babe helped.

Each time we stuck ourselves on the thorns we got sadder. By the time we'd done, we were in the right mood for a funeral.

We knelt down beside Bob and helped him shuck the petals from the flowers. Then everything was ready. Dora wasn't around. James said she was locked in the garage with the pups. She wasn't coming to the funeral.

"Why not?" I asked. "She's their mother. When Jerry Rice fell through th' ice an' got drowned in th' creek his mother was at th' funeral!"

"Yeah," Bob admitted, "but she didn' try ta dig him up. Dora would. That'd spoil everythin'."

We held the funeral without her. We were about to start services when Mr. and Mrs. Scott came out of the house. He was going to work. They looked our way and we suspended everything for the moment. Mrs. Scott's eyes widened.

"*My God!*" she said. "*My flowers!*"

"Mary, Mary," Mr. Scott said, taking in the situation at a glance. "Haven't you ever been to a funeral? They have to have flowers! You can grow more." He kissed her and told her to go back in the house. Then he went off down the street.

It was a close shave and it took us a second or two to get back in the mood. We could hear Mrs. Scott in the house, banging things around and talking to herself.

But then the perfume drifted up from the rose petals.

"How do we start?" Bob asked.

Babe burst into tears. He got up off his knees and went over and flung himself down on the grass, sobbing bitterly, undone by grief.

"Pray, I guess," I said.

"You start," James said.

"I don't wanta say anythin', in English," I said.

"Any which way, go ahead," he agreed.

Bob nodded.

I cupped my hands in front of my mouth.

"*Inna ilahi w' inna ilaihi rajighun—Janlari jannatda bulsun . . .*"

"Amen," James said.

"How about th' Lord's Prayer now?" Bob asked.

"All right," James said. He turned to me. "Lord's Prayer okay with you?"

"Sure," I said.

We bowed our heads again. James repeated the prayer. I could feel the sorrow rise up in me.

"*Our Father who art in heaven, hallowed be Thy name,*
Thy kingdom come, Thy will be done,
On earth, as it is in heaven.
Give us this day our daily bread,
And forgive us our trespasses—
As we forgive those who trespass against us.
Lead us not into temptation, but deliver us from evil,
For thine is the Kingdom, and the Power, and the Glory.
Amen."

We straightened.

"Now you say somethin'," James said to Bob.

"Uh-uh," Bob said.

"You gotta."

Bob took a little while. He looked at the mound of rose petals and wiped his nose on his sleeve.

"Well," he said, "I c'n think of two guys who're gonna wish they din't *trespass* against us—if it kills me!"

"Now you, in English," James said to me.

"What Bob said, *double!*" I said. "Amen!"

We got off our knees and went into the garage and patted Dora and looked at the pups. Babe got up from the grass and tagged along. One of the pups was mostly black with a few white spots. The other was mostly white with a few black spots. They'd grown overnight. They were eating for ten.

"We gotta make money fast," James said. "After we get dog tags, Bert an' Jimmy won't dare touch 'em."

"Four bucks," Bob said.

Babe hicupped.

"Think we c'n leave Dora an' her pups here, alone?" I asked. "Mightn't *they* come back? Your pop's gone to work."

"He's bad when he's mad," James said. "But he don't do anythin' much, jus' rampage around. Mom's different· She's liable ta do most anythin'. She gets excited. Seein' them dead pups las' night after Bert an' Jimmy run— seein' that set her in a state!"

Bob nodded.

"When she's in a state," James continued, "she's dangerous as all get-out. She said *fiends* three times."

"Ta herself," Bob added, "soft-like. 'At's awful bad."

"Them bastids come around here—" James declared, "they come anywheres near Dora an' th' pups, an' Mom'll lambast 'em with anythin' comes ta hand!"

Bob stood in silent agreement.

"Okay," I said. "Only, Babe better stand guard. He c'n yell if they come around. Then she c'n come tearin' out."

"I wanna go along with you guys." Babe hicupped, still wet-eyed from the funeral.

"Ya want th' rest a' th' puppies murdered?" James asked.

Babe shook his head, half sobbing at the very thought.

"Then ya gotta be sentry!"

Babe was convinced. He got the garbage can and hauled it over in front of the garage and sat on it.

"Pazhazhazha!" he said, defying an imaginary foe.

We locked the garage door just to be on the safe side. Then we took the coaster wagon and went to my house. We loaded the diving rig into it and went across Lake Shore Boulevard and on down toward the cliff that fronted the beach. We had our bathing suits on under our clothes.

※※※

Lake Erie was quiet and there weren't any bathers out yet. It was too early in the morning. Bob pointed to a stretch of private beach this side of the amusement park; there were homes set back from the lake so that the pressure ice in the winter wouldn't crush them. Each house had a couple of rowboats or canoes upside down on the sand.

James and I worked the wagon down to the rocky beach while Bob went to get a boat. A *rowboat*, I said, no canoes! It looked to me as though I was elected to do most of the diving, at least in the beginning—until the twins were satisfied it wasn't going to drown them—and I didn't want them to turn over in a canoe and lose the pump while I was on the bottom of the lake gathering fishhooks.

We got down to the water's edge and sat down and waited for Bob. James didn't seem very concerned. I looked at the hot-water heater helmet and wabbled the pump handle. It was tight. We could hear the air hiss.

"Whatcha worryin' about?" James asked.

"I ain't worryin'," I said.

"Ya look worried," he insisted.

"Well, I ain't!" I denied.

"It worked in th' ditch," James said.

I looked out across the lake. It vanished into a watery horizon.

"Sixty miles across th' lake ta Canada," I said.

"So what?" James sneered. "Ya ain't goin' ta Canada. What's th' matter? Ya got goose bumps all over!"

We'd undressed when we got to the beach. I looked at my goose bumps.

"It ain't cold," James said. "I ain't got none."

"I had cold milk fer breakfast," I explained, feeling trapped. "My mother made me drink it."

James sneered again.

"I got some ice off'n th' ice wagon a coupla days ago. It didn' give me no goose bumps!"

I leaped to my feet and made my hands into fists, goaded beyond endurance.

"You're jus' beggin' fer a scab on yer nose!" I yelled. "C'mon, stand up!"

James got up and hit me squarely in the eye. I staggered back and sat down. I sprang up again and rushed him and popped him in the eye and we went down together. In that instant two things happened: Bob shouted and a stone clanged off the helmet.

James and I stopped struggling and looked around.

Bob was coming around the rock breakwater in a green rowboat. He yelled again and pointed. Another stone thudded into the sand close to us. We looked up in the direction Bob pointed.

Bert and Jimmy were on the cliffs. It was a two- or three-minute climb down the cliff path and they saw that we'd be gone before they got to us. They came anyhow, heaving rocks at us all the time. James got beaned and went into a fury, jumping up and down and holding his head.

Then Bob got to the shore and we hurried at loading the stuff before the Coffees got there. We got everything into the boat, everything except the coaster wagon. We had to leave it. Bert and Jimmy were almost on us and rocks were falling like rain.

Quite as Ulysses with the Cyclops, we pushed away from the shore and rowed for all we were worth. James got beaned again and punched Bob in the mouth for not rowing faster. Then I rowed all alone while they fought in the bottom of the boat. I kept rowing until we were out of range.

When Bert and Jimmy saw that we couldn't be reached, they concentrated on the wagon. They busted it all to pieces. They picked it up and hurled it down. They got big rocks and dropped them on it. They even bashed up the wheels. Then, when the destruction was complete, when there wasn't anything more they could do, they heaved the wreckage into the lake.

"Holy Smoke!" James said, dumbfounded. "What'll Pop say?"

"He give it ta us fer Christmas a coupla years back," Bob said. The fight between the twins had stopped when I yelled that the coaster wagon was being busted up.

We yelled threats back and forth between the drifting boat and the shore for a while, then we in the boat rowed past the fence that jutted out into the water separating the public beach from the amusement park. When they saw where we were headed, the Coffees ran back up the cliffs and disappeared. There was no way of getting over the fence and into the park; if they wanted to follow us they would have to go around to the entrance at the corner of Lake Shore Boulevard.

All of us in the boat had black eyes. And James had an extra two big lumps on his head where the hair stood up straight. But we felt good. All except for the wagon. The air was warm and exhilarating. The water was calm and glistening. I had one oar and James took the other. We sat on the single thwart, side by side, and Bob called the stroke.

We rowed way out on the lake and had a lot of fun with the rowboat. It was a dandy. It was made of canvas stretched over a wooden strip frame and painted; it was light and easy to handle. But the helmet kept looking at us. And it reminded us of the pups.

At last we couldn't stall any longer. We started for the pier.

The amusement park was quiet. It didn't open for business until the afternoon. There were a few people wandering around and looking at the roller-coaster trestles and the hanging airplanes that flew around in circles when the power was on. But everything was pretty sleepy. Once we heard a few shots from the direction of the shooting gallery; when they died away there weren't any more.

There were a few people fishing from the pier. The regulars. They didn't pay any attention to us.

"I guess them bastids went home," James said. The

Coffee boys weren't anywhere to be seen. They'd had plenty of time to put in an appearance.

"Think th' pups're safe?" I asked. "Maybe we should oughta go look?"

"They're safe!" James yelled. "Gettin' worried again?"

"Yella?" Bob asked, rowing harder. James and I had given him the oars.

"Maybe we should test it more," I hedged, "before doin' any serious divin'."

"Yer gonna test it!" James said.

"How ya figger on testin' it without divin'?" Bob wanted to know.

I couldn't think of anything to say.

We rowed the length of the pier to within fifty feet of the beach, then worked the rowboat between the pilings and into the gloom underneath. There was a jungle of pilings all around us, marching out another couple of hundred feet to the outer end. We'd planned it this way. We couldn't be seen by anybody up above. The Coffees would never find us—and, if they did, they wouldn't be able to get at us.

We stopped rowing and looked at one another. Bob shipped the oars and tied the boat to one of the piles. It was eerie down there.

Bob got back to the thwart and lifted one of the oars out of the oarlock and stuck it down into the water. It disappeared entirely. His arms were submerged up to the shoulders and his chin was touching the water before he fetched bottom.

He lifted the oar back into the boat. The twins looked at me. I looked at the water. All the merriment went out of life.

"Well," James demanded, "ya gonna do it, or ain'cha?"

"It's kinda deep," I said.

"We gotta get dog tags," Bob said. "If you won't, I will!"

"*No ya won't!*" I declared, challenged. "It's my idea. *I go first!*"

Bob sighed with relief. I'd stuck my neck out.

We coiled up the lifeline and tied one end to the fitting on top of the helmet, with a hunk left over to put around me under the armpits. Then I reconsidered and decided that I didn't care to be tied to anything. I could always abandon the helmet and swim to the surface, but if I got the rope fouled, and me fastened to it, I might swallow a lot of water before I got free.

We lowered the helmet over the stern of the boat and Bob wabbled the pump. The tire pumps, four, were fastened to a plank, two pumps on either side, opposing each other. As he worked the handle the beer hose writhed and stiffened. The helmet got lighter in the water.

The air hissed into it and it got still lighter. Then bubbles started to erupt from the shoulder slots.

"Hot diggety dog!" James said. "She's fulla air."

"Hang on," I said. I lowered myself over the side of

the rowboat. In up to my armpits, I let go. The water under the pier was cold, but I wasn't afraid any more. It was because of the twins' faces. Now, suddenly, at the last minute, they were riddled with envy.

I took a breath and sank down under the helmet and came up inside—and breathed. Air. It smelled of oil, from the pumps, and of rubber, from the hose, but it was genuine air. I fastened the arm loops and hung there, beneath the boat. I could see out of the faceplate. I was looking forward and could see the entire keel to where it curled up to make the prow. I saw pilings ten or fifteen feet away. And I saw the bottom—the bottom of the lake!

I freed myself of the helmet, sank from under it, and broke the surface.

I got hold of the gunwale and hung there, panting from excitement.

"Wha's it like?" James asked, equally excited, hanging on to the helmet rope a little tighter. Bob had stopped pumping. *"Wha's it like?* Does it work okay, huh?"

"Say somethin'!" Bob demanded. He started pulling off his clothes; he hadn't undressed before. "It's my turn!"

"I haven't gone down yet!" I yelled. "Now I get fishhooks. Drop that anchor over here so's I c'n go down th' rope."

"What for?"

"Dope," James said, "tha's th' way it said ta do in th' magazine!"

Bob scrambled over the thwart and got the concrete

117

block anchor out of the bow. He lugged it to the stern and put it over. He stepped on James and they almost got into a fight—except that James couldn't turn loose from the helmet rope.

"Shut up, you guys!" I commanded. "*Pump!*" Bob grinned and started pumping. I submerged.

I got under the helmet and took hold of the anchor rope. The helmet settled on my shoulders. James was paying out line. I was on my way down.

It was only about ten feet of water, but it seemed like a week's journey. The helmet was heavy and pressed me toward the bottom, but I clung to the anchor rope for dear life, descending slowly.

I was just beginning to get frightened at the weight of the water on my body, and the chill, when I stubbed my toe on the bottom. Still clinging to the rope, I leaned back a little and looked up. It wasn't so far to the surface. And the water wasn't as dark as it had seemed to be. But it was a lot spookier than squatting in a ditch! I let go of the rope.

Staying well in the shadow of the pier, far enough back so that the escaping air bubbles wouldn't be seen by anybody fishing, I worked from piling to piling, I got fishhooks all right—and the yield would get better if we could work out near the end of the pier where most of the fishing was done and most of the lines lost.

I got eight fishhooks, eleven sinkers, a rusted reel that still worked, a first-class lunch bucket with a bloated pickle inside, a pair of smoked spectacles, and a two-bit piece. And I saw fish. They came and looked at me, got wrought up, rushed away, and then came back for another look. Both of us were astonished. It was great. I felt like twenty-thousand leagues under the sea.

I was squatting to pick up the two-bits—there was no bending over, the air would rush out *bloop* and the helmet would fill instantly if it was tilted from the vertical—I'd learned that much in the irrigation ditch—when, suddenly, the air stopped coming down to me. Water started rising in the helmet.

I stood up and my heart pounded. The pump had stopped.

I was about to shed the helmet and swim up when the air went *sst—sst—sst—sst* again and I felt a warm breath blow against the top of my head. They were pumping again. I was getting cold.

I relocated the two-bits, put my big toe on it, squatted, and got it. Then the air stopped again. It stayed stopped. I shed the helmet and swam to the surface with my hands full. I'd been down about fifteen minutes.

"Hey!" I yelled, still in the water, "what's a'matter with you guys? Ya can't stop pumpin' with a diver on 'th bottom of a lake!"

I didn't get much attention, even when I got to the side of the rowboat and threw the stuff in. The twins were jumping around in the boat, looking up at the bottom of the pier.

"Hey," I yelled again, shivering, "you guys *nuts?* Ya can't stop pumpin' like that!"

"So's yer ole man!" James shouted at me. "You ain't been spit on like we have! Them guys're up there on top spittin' on us!" He and Bob went back to yelling insults at the floor of the pier. My ears cleared and I could hear some muffled yells from above. Then a spray of saliva descended on Bob. I could see one set of eyes and another set of lips framed in one of the cracks between the timbers. Then they shifted. Another two eyes sighted on us and another two lips let go. Bob got it again. The Coffee boys had located us.

We got the helmet up and pushed along between the pilings until we got to a place where the floor above was solid; there, no longer in danger of being spit on, I showed the twins what I'd salvaged. I had it all in the lunch bucket. Then I showed them the two-bit piece. That made them feel better. When I told them I'd seen fish down there and they'd swum right up to me, the twins forgot about Bert and Jimmy.

Bob went down. James watched the beer hose and line and I pumped. Then, while the Coffees thumped around overhead, trying to find some way to plague us, and failing, we made a big haul. Bob started bringing up old milk bottles. I hadn't thought of that and I'd seen plenty. The people who fished used them to keep bait in; in the course of years any number had gotten knocked off the edge of the pier. Now, every minute or so, Bob would break the surface with a bottle in each hand. We'd take them from him—two cents each—haul up the helmet, he'd get under it, and down again.

We had about thirty milk bottles in the boat when we heard Mr. Coffee's voice. His boys had called him.

"GET OUTTA THERE!" he bellowed, hanging his head over the edge of the pier deck and looking upside down at us. He was in his uniform. *"GET OUTTA THERE! Yer unner arrest, all of ya! No swimmin' allowed under th' pier!"*

"G'wan," James yelled, "arrest yer own kids, them murderers. They spit on us."

"YER UNNER ARREST!" Mr. Coffee bellowed again. "C'mon outta there!"

Bob broke the surface with a milk bottle in one hand, the other empty.

"Ain't any more down there," he panted, blue around the lips, "le's move on down a little." He shivered and noticed Mr. Coffee and his boys looking at us upside down.

"He says we're unner arrest fer swimmin'," James explained.

"Ain't swimmin'," Bob said, shivering again.

"C'MON OUT!" Mr. Coffee thundered.

"Lookit his face, all purple," James said.

"It's unhealthy," I commented, "bein' upside down so long."

"Vein'll bust," Bob said, getting into the boat.

"They stole th' boat!" one of the Coffees yelled. "Them thieves!"

"They smashed up our wagon an' chucked it in th' lake!" I countered.

"*Yer unnER arrEST!*" Mr. Coffee shrieked, his voice cracked from being upside down so long. "*FER thEFt!*"

"We barra'd it," James said; he sounded worried.

"Shut up," Bob said, nudging him. "They're nuts. Gimme a hand here."

Mr. Coffee pulled up his head and disappeared. We worked the rowboat farther out from shore, still keeping well under the pier. We had about forty people interested by this time—everybody upside down and looking at us. One of them was the old lady who'd gotten mad at Bob and James when they asked what she'd give for a deep-sea diver to get her catgut leader and hooks and sinkers back. We looked up at her. "*Well, I swan!*" she declared, recognizing us.

When we stopped again, it was Bob's turn to pump. James looked back toward the foot of the pier. It was getting far away. It was James's turn to go down. He was game; he slipped over the side and got ready. There was a dog running around up on top. I heard the pattering of its paws. And it whined. That bothered me. I didn't say anything to the twins. The Coffees couldn't have gotten past Mrs. Scott. I wouldn't even consider it.

"Bottom don't slope hardly at all," I told James. While I was down we'd worked out to about fourteen feet. From then on the depth had been constant. "We got no more anchor rope over than we had before."

But it wasn't the depth that worried James as much as the yelling and the audience. There were grown-ups and kids, men and women—all asking what we were doing, and asking us what it was like down under water; some of them telling us to get out of there before we killed ourselves; and some telling us how to dive; and one man wanting us to look for his fountain pen which he'd lost a few weeks back.

"*Get plenty milk bottles,*" I whispered to James. "Get anythin' worth money. Somethin' tells me we won't be comin' around here much after t'day."

Bob nodded and said: "Milk bottles. All we gotta do is take 'em ta a grocery store. Get bottles."

James sank. He got under the helmet and I gave him a chance to get organized. Then I paid out rope and air hose and lowered away.

Mr. Coffee put his head over again.

Bob said: "Hey, ya look better fer havin' walked around a while."

"Ya ain't so purple as before," I said.

James had just reached bottom when the beer hose blew off the top of the helmet. I saw it whip up to the surface, squirming and sputtering. Bob fell over the pump as the pressure suddenly vanished. A thin stream of bubbles came up from the bottom, where James was. The helmet was emptying itself through the valve in the top, where the hose blew off. We waited, but James didn't come up.

Bob looked at me.

I went over.

James was still standing there, still in the helmet, look-ing surprised. He was still holding on to the anchor rope. As I looked in through the faceplate, Bob started to take up the helmet. I got hold of James and woke him up. He helped me to get him to the surface, then he grabbed hold of the gunwale, choking and coughing.

"Yer unner arrest!" Mr. Coffee said.

His kids had their heads over the edge of the pier again.

"Boy, oh, boy!" Bert yelled. "Are you guys gonna catch it! Pop called yer ole man on th' telephone. He's left th' gas station an' comin' right over!"

James stopped coughing and wheezed a couple times. We looked at Mr. Coffee. It was true! Bob's eyes got big. He looked at the tire pumps.

"C'mon," he yelled; he helped us out of the water. The anchor rope had gotten twisted around a piling as the boat drifted. We couldn't untwist it fast enough for Bob. He threw the rest of the rope overboard.

"Hey, don't do that!" one of the spectators yelled. We looked up. It was another upside-down face, sort of old. He'd been watching us for quite a while. He had a little gray beard.

"Nuts!" Bob said. "Crimeny, if Pop sees them pumps . . ."

He started rowing as James and I struggled to get the

helmet aboard. We got it up to the gunwale when James started coughing again and let go and mashed my fingers between the helmet and the boat. Then Bob ran us slam-bang into a piling and the helmet came aboard and onto James's foot and we went down into the bottom of the boat with a crash of broken milk bottles.

The oars thrashed around in the water as Bob got us going again. We were still under the pier.

"Go easy with that boat!" shouted the guy with the beard.

"*Stop, you liTTLe thiEVEs!*" Mr. Coffee screeched, seeing we were about to make a get-away, his voice breaking again. "*Take thAT bOAt IN!*"

"Nuts!" Bob said again, desperately ricocheting off a couple more pilings.

"Thieves! *Thieves!* THIEVES! *THIEVES!*" yelled Bert and Jimmy.

"Le's get out from unner th' pier!" I yelled.

"Whatcha think I'm tryin' ta do?" Bob screamed, drag-ging at the oars and gaining momentum.

"Gosh a'mighty," James gasped, in pain, "lookit my foot! Lookit what you done when ya pulled th' helmet on me. I'm bleedin'!"

We slammed into another piling and Bob went over onto his back with his bare feet waving around in the air. As he struggled up an oar handle caught him in the mouth and flipped him over again. "*Jeez!*" he said. I would have moved forward and taken the oars, but there were too many broken milk bottles between me and the rowing thwart. Some of the upside-down faces laughed.

As Bob got us going again I began throwing over hunks of broken milk bottles. James coughed and wheezed and groaned beside me, babying his skinned foot, rocking himself back and forth.

"*Bert! JIM!*" Mr. Coffee yelled upside down across the bottom of the pier, they were on opposite sides. "Where'd that rowboat come from? Who owns it?"

"They stole it from 'at house down th' lake," Bert yelled back.

"We saw 'em," Jimmy added.

"It's *my* boat," said the guy with the beard. "I've been following along the shore. I live there."

"*Jeez!*" Bob said again, dragging at the oars with all his might. Just one more line of pilings separated us from the open lake. We'd really begun to move.

"We're takin' it back right now, Mister," I said.

James stopped rocking himself back and forth and blowing on his foot and asked me: "How far'd ya say it was t' Canada?"

"LOOK OUT!" I yelled to Bob, but it was too late. We slithered along a pile that had a big rusty, corroded spike sticking out of it. The jagged iron gouged through the canvas from stem to stern and took off about half of the boat.

"*Jeez!*" Bob gasped as he watched the water gush in.

"Jus' like bein' in a war," James said, awed, and forgetting his foot.

"*Oh!*" said the man with the beard. We were right under him.

"We'll fix it, Mister," I said.

Bob kept trying to row. We were clear of the pier and headed out into the lake. Our shoes, all three pairs, were floating half-submerged back under the pier. Our clothing was there too. It had been stowed in the torn-out side and the spike had pulled it out. James grabbed one sock before it drifted out of reach. He put it on. Then he looked back at the pier and the shore. The rowboat was filling.

"Wait!" he yelled at Bob. "Don't go out any more!" We were about three hundred feet from the beach. "I can't swim that far!"

"Me, neither," Bob grunted, rowing. "Whaddya wanta swim fer? We go back there an' Pop sees these pumps an' he'll murder us. An'—when he gets through—'at guy with th' funny face'll give us th' 'lectric chair!"

I was thinking of what my mother was going to do to me when they called her up from the jail. She'd probably decide she wasn't strong enough and ask Mr. Scott to deal with me. That was the very least she'd do.

James scrunched over close to me so that the water wouldn't come in so fast. Already we were three-quarters sunk. Maybe nine-tenths. Milk bottles were floating all around. Even the two-bits was gone. It had gone down with the lunch bucket and fishhooks; they'd been on the bottom part that was ripped off.

Everybody who had been on the other side of the pier came running across to get a better look at us. Then I saw the dog I'd heard running around up above. *It was Dora!* She was following Jimmy and whining. . . .

"Throw th' pumps an' helmet overboard," Bob yelled. "Maybe we c'n make it around th' other side of th' fence."

"*There's* Dora," I said. "An' Jimmy's got our pups. They went an' got 'em after throwin' rocks at us."

"*What?*" Bob said. He looked. James looked. Jimmy had a pup in each hand. He held them out and showed them to us, triumphant. Dora was hysterical.

Then, very suddenly, very gently, the rowboat sank and we were swimming in the midst of a flotilla of milk bottles.

There was only one place to go: to a ladder that went up from the water at the end of the pier. We got there all at the same time. There was no use in our staying down below. We had to go up some time. We rescued as much of our clothing as hadn't already sunk.

⋙⋘

Mr. Coffee grabbed us as we came over the top and onto the pier deck. He got us one by one, shook us, squeezed our arms hard, and handed us to another park attendant. We didn't struggle and we didn't raise our eyes. Losing the pups had been the last straw.

128

The man with the beard stepped in and made Mr. Coffee stop pushing us around. Mr. Coffee grabbed him by the shoulder and was about to give him a shove when the little old guy said slowly: "Take your hands off me, lout!"

"Mind yer own business, you character, you!" Mr. Coffee yelled into his face, but not shoving. "These here brats're goin' ta Juvenile Hall!"

"Bad Boy School," Bert translated, grinning.

"Mister," I made a last appeal to the man with the beard, "please, sir, we're sorry about your boat. They killed our pups, all except th' two Jimmy's got there. We were tryin' ta make some money for dog licenses—fer th' two we had left . . ."

"So's they wouldn' get murdered too," James said.

"I took th' boat, sir," Bob said, "on a loan."

"They killed your puppies?" the man asked.

"Eight!" Bob said, beginning to cry, half in mortification—by this time we had a good seventy-five or eighty persons in the audience—half in sorrow, and half because he expected his father along any second, and the plank with the pumps fastened to it was floating around in full sight of everyone, seventy feet of red beer hose trailing after it.

"Eight puppies?" the man asked.

"Yes, sir," I said. "Murdered!"

"Who did?"

"They did!" The twins and I pointed at the Coffees, including Mr. Coffee. He got red. He grabbed hold of my arm and hurt it.

"C'mon!" he ordered, starting to haul me away.

"*Just a minute!*" the bearded man said. "I want to hear some more of this." Some other people did too. They said so. "Turn loose of the boy, officer."

"I won't run away," I said.

"*Who* killed your puppies?"

"They're liars," Bert said. "They was ours."

"You killed them?"

"Yeah," Jimmy made a face. "What's it to ya? Our old man said we could. They was ours!" He shut up when he saw his father's face.

"Their mom gave us th' pups," James explained, beginning to sniffle; he'd noticed the pumps floating around. "So's they wouldn' kill 'em. They stole 'em back an' murdered eight out in front a' our house. Right while Dora watched: their mother!"

"That's her over there, scared about th' pups Jimmy's holdin'," I said, pointing, and gritting my teeth. The tears were contagious.

Everybody looked at Dora.

"We was tryin' ta make some money fer dog tags so they couldn' ever touch th' two that was left—so's they'd be ours, legal," James said.

"We had thirty milk bottles," Bob said, eyes narrowing.

130

"An' eight fishhooks, eleven sinkers, an' some other stuff—an' a quarter, cash!" I said. "All sunk!"

"Give us back our pups!" Bob demanded of Jimmy.

"They'll just kill 'em as soon as nobody's lookin'," said James, appealing to the man with the beard. "Their eyes aren't even open yet. Look, they're jus' babies."

"Give them to them," said the man, making up his mind.

"Don't do it, son!" said Mr. Coffee.

Jimmy turned and threw both pups into the lake. Everybody gasped.

"You're suspended, sir!" said the bearded man to Mr. Coffee.

Then I hit the water. A belly whopper. It was a ten- or twelve-foot dive from the pier. James and Bob were in the water with me. So was a girl about twenty, all dressed. And so was Dora.

Up on the pier everybody was boiling mad.

The girl got one of the pups and Bob got the other. Then we climbed up the ladder. A man came down and got Dora.

"Who're you, you character, you?" demanded Mr. Coffee for a second time.

"My name's Randolph," said the man with the beard, "and you're suspended!"

The park attendant who'd been helping Mr. Coffee stepped back into the crowd. He seemed to have recognized the name. Mr. Coffee had heard of Mr. Randolph. He looked as if he'd swallowed something hot and unpleasant.

"They're dead," wailed the girl who'd jumped in with her clothes on, "both of them. They were too young . : ."

The wet puppies were flattened out on the rough pier planks and Dora was licking them and whining. Her tail was between her legs.

Bob squealed and made a leap for Jimmy Coffee. He nailed him. Jimmy hit back and Bob went down. I stepped in and punched Bert in the belly and got konked on the ear in return. James took my place. By the time he was down, I was up. A woman cried out for someone to stop it. Mr. Randolph said for her to take it easy.

Then Mr. Scott arrived. He pushed through the crowd to where he could see what was taking place and shouted for James and Bob to stop immediately! He was boiling.

"Please, sir," said Mr. Randolph, "this is an affair of honor. I wouldn't interfere."

"I'm their father!" shouted Mr. Scott. "Who're you?"

"You should be proud," said Mr. Randolph. He sighed. "My name's Randolph. They're outmatched, but they've got a cause—and they've got inspiration."

"I voted for you," said Mr. Scott, calming a little.

Mr. Coffee got paler.

"Thank you," said the man with the beard. "Now, shall we proceed? Step back, everybody. Give them some room."

It lasted about five minutes. And it was strenuous; almost as bad as last time. People kept saying to stop it.

Mr. Randolph replied that this was the one time in his life that he'd had the opportunity to let virtue triumph over evil. He sermonized as we fought. He calmed the others. He said—I heard about it later—that the dark forces were very strong in this world. If they weren't, he said, it wouldn't be worth a man's while and efforts to defeat them.

"Friends," he said as I got walloped again, "please, let us today see if virtue can of itself triumph?"

It almost didn't.

Mr. Scott began to rub his jaw, and he had to turn aside a couple times. He couldn't bear to look. Then, just as Mr. Randolph shook his head and was about to step in and stop it, I got Jimmy a good one, right on the kisser. I connected strictly from luck. The twins and I were getting so punchy by this time that frequently we swung wide and hit one another. I had a fat ear that Bob had given me. Jimmy went down. He bumped his head on the pier deck. He got up with a roar and I clunked him again. It was like one of those things in a dream. He sprawled on the planks.

Then Bert went down. Bob did it. They had plenty of spunk, the Coffee kids; they had too much; they kept right on fighting when we had them whipped. They almost won that way. Then I got Jimmy again and he didn't get up. He just sat there all puffed and swollen and discolored, ignoring me, and feeling under his nose to see how much blood he was losing.

"Get outta my way—" Bob yelled at James, thrusting him aside.

James and I stood back and watched Bob whittle Bert down to his size, then chop him off.

"Hallelujah!" Mr. Randolph said when it was over.

Just then Mr. Daniels showed up in the crowd and yelled: "Them hooligans! Hold 'em! They're the ones stole my rubber hose. Seventy feet!"

"Which ones?" Mr. Randolph asked.

"Them three," said Mr. Daniels, pointing to us. We were so beat up and blown that we could hardly stand.

"They took it in the form of a loan, sir, I'm sure," said Mr. Randolph.

"*Loan!*" yelled Mr. Daniels. "Look at it out there in the water. I can't take that back in my drugstore!"

"No?" mused Mr. Randolph. "No? Well, I suppose you can't. In that case we'll just consider it as contributed to a worthy cause. I donated a very good boat. Made it myself."

Someone in the crowd said something to Mr. Daniels and he shut up. Mr. Randolph seemed very happy. Mr. Scott didn't; he'd just spotted his missing tire pumps floating around out there on the lake.

Then Dora yelped. One of the pups was trying to get into her fur. *It was alive.*

But the black pup with the white spots was quiet. It never moved again. James and Bob and I hunkered down beside Dora and calmed her a little. She growled when the Coffees came close.

A voice from the crowd told them: "Get outa here, you. All of ya! G'wan, beat it!"

"That," nodded Mr. Randolph, looking at Mr. Coffee and his sons, "perfectly expresses the opinion of the majority. Take heed and depart."

Mr. Coffee got purple again, but he didn't utter a word. They went away. Dora stopped growling.

"What will you name him?" asked Mr. Randolph.

James couldn't speak. He had the dead pup in his arms. I couldn't think.

Bob spoke up: "Sir," he said, stroking Dora, "we'd like ta name him Randolph, out of respect fer you."

Mr. Randolph pulled his nose and smoothed his short beard. Some people laughed. Some didn't. Mr. Randolph nodded.

"Thank you—all," he said. "I don't know that I've ever been so honored. Now take my godchild home before it catches a chill."

The crowd let us through. Mr. Randolph stopped Mr. Scott and asked for his address. Mr. Scott was beginning to smile, even though his pumps were floating around. Somebody gave us a turkish towel and we wrapped Randolph in it and went ahead, Dora running beside us.

>>><<<

We found out how Bert and Jimmy had gotten the pups. After throwing rocks at us, they'd run back to the Scott house to see if they could recover Dora and her surviving babies. Mrs. Scott was in the backyard, hanging wash. She'd opened the garage to get some clothespins. Myrtle had come around and Babe left his sentry post to get two chairs and a blanket to make a house. While Bert and Jimmy stole back the pups, he and Myrtle were playing papa and mama underneath the two chairs and blanket. Dora and the pups were gone when Mrs. Scott returned. She thought we'd taken them.

We made a second little grave beside the other one and lay the dead pup to rest with his brothers and sisters. We scattered more flower petals. We got them from the garden next door.

The tension was gone. The Coffees didn't dare to come around. Their old man was afraid that if they caused any more trouble, his suspension never would be lifted.

The next morning a police car pulled up in front of the Scott house and a cop said he wanted to see three kids: he had an envelope for them. Myrtle came and told me; I was still eating my breakfast. She yelled to hurry up, that James and Bob couldn't wait to open it.

It held a dog tag. Mr. Randolph had worked fast. On the back of the tag someone had stamped *RANDOLPH*.

⨯⨯⨯ *12* ⨯⨯⨯

Beauty and the Beast

R ANDOLPH kept us pretty busy. The summer just
galloped away.

School opened again. And there were concerts again.
The first concert we were taken to, Mr. Eddy kept a
hawk eye on us. James, Bob, and me. So did Mrs. Eddy—
the same Miss Roth, only a bit fatter, and a lot warmer.
They were just wasting their time. We liked music. We
just sat there, spellbound, remembering.

Randolph did it. He'd taught us to appreciate the finer
things in life.

Music is created of curious things. Of mechanisms. It
is a dust-dry pattern; a chill technique; a metallic timing.
And proficiency—an unyielding, correct, brittle thing.

Music matters only when it is a sudden aroma in the
nostrils, a sudden taste upon the tongue, a sudden joy in
the heart, and a sudden anguish in the bone. Music is a

memory. Music is feminine. Music is a woman. Once this is known, the mechanisms become lips, trembling, or smiling, silent, or speaking; sullen, pouting; whispering, lulling—and suddenly provoking and shocking! The dust-dry pattern becomes a gesture, a hand touching and withdrawing—to touch again. The chill technique alters, is transformed: it is a trusting, and mistrusting. The metallic timing is a knowing, an impatience, a wanting what has been wanted many times before, and to be wanted many times again, a having. And the proficiency is a step, a way of walking; a look, a way of watching; a desire, a way of satisfying; a pain, a way of hurting. Music is wanton.

Music is a virgin standing by the water's edge. Music is a secret kept because there are no words for the telling. All unthinking, Randolph had taught us these things.

>∗∗∗<

Randolph was exactly two months and three weeks old and school was almost upon us when we decided to take him out to Mentor Marsh. We decided it in the clubhouse. It was about eight o'clock in the morning, but we'd been there a good hour already. Bob and James and I were eating graham crackers and feeding little bits to Randolph. Otherwise we were silent. It was Monday. In one week we'd be in a classroom again. There was an epidemic of chicken-pox in Cleveland and the reopening of school had been set back a week. If there'd been no epidemic, we'd have been starting this very day.

Already the smell of education was in our nostrils: the combined aromas, odors, reeks, and stinks of ink, tablet paper, pulverized carbon and pencil wood from overflowing pencil sharpeners, eraser rubbings, chalk dust, the newly silvered steam radiators the first time they were turned on, and the stuff the janitor used on the floors after we went home.

Bob took the last graham cracker and split it four ways. Then we gave Randolph the empty box to sniff, so that he wouldn't think we were holding out on him.

"Lord!" James said, looking at the sky. "I hate it. I jus' hate it!"

"Days gettin' shorter now," I said. "Pretty soon th' leaves'll be droppin' off th' trees."

"Sound of chalk squeakin' against a blackboard makes my teeth stick out," Bob said, digging a hole in the clubhouse floor.

"That don't bother me," I said, patting Randolph. "What gets me is th' feel of a felt eraser against my fingers an' rubbin' it against a slate, dry. If it was wet it wouldn' be so bad."

"What I can't look at is Irene," James said. "Always chewin' on th' corner of a handkerchief!" He spit between his knees. "How c'n a *human bein'* put cloth against her teeth?"

"6B—6A," Bob figured, "after this semester we'll be graduated ta Junior High."

"Six—seven—eight—nine—ten—eleven—twelve— *Lord!*" James said, counting on his fingers. "Six, no, *seven* more years of goin' ta school. Then college. Pop says we gotta go ta college!"

The enormity of it overwhelmed us.

"Le's us go out ta Mentor Marsh?" I suggested. "Huh?"

"Le's go," Bob said, getting up.

We started early enough, but Babe came out of the house just as we were crossing toward the boulevard. We had a little difficulty getting rid of him. Then we couldn't get a ride. We walked quite a distance. At last we crawled into a parked banana truck. The driver didn't discover us until he was under way and three or four miles up the road.

"What th' . . ." he yelled. "Ya can't ride on this truck! Din't you kids see th' sign up here: NO RIDERS, din't ya?" He spoke to us through the back window of the cab; it was broken. We were in the covered bed of the truck, with the bananas. The driver stepped on the brakes. "When ya get on, anyhow?"

"Back there, by th' grocery store," I said. "We thought you wouldn't care. We got a pup here an' he was tired walkin'."

"We thought th' sign meant in front, with you," Bob said.

"I'll bet!" the man said.

"We hiked all th' way from Euclid Beach," James added. The truck was easing to a stop. "Our pup's paws hurt."

"Pup?" the man said. "Th' hell you say!" The truck kept rolling; he'd let up on the brake. "Hold 'im up. I c'n see 'im in th' rear-view mirror."

I held Randolph up.

"See?"

"Funny little roly-poly bugger," the man said. "How long ya had 'im?"

"Almost ever since he was born," James said.

"Where ya takin' 'im?"

"Mentor Marsh—fishin'," I explained.

"Hold 'im up again," the man yelled over his shoulder, keeping his eye on the mirror that was fastened over the windshield for looking straight back through the truck.

I held Randolph up again. He smiled. He liked being held up. He thought it was a game.

"Y'say his feet hurt?"

"He was limpin' on all four feet," James said. "It looked awful. We been walkin' since after breakfast."

"Why din't ya carry 'im?" the man asked.

"He don't like it," I said. "He likes to smell things up close."

"Oh," the man said. The truck gained a little speed. Bob and James and I looked over the stalks of bananas.

"Listen," the truck driver said. "Anythin' c'n happen— an' usually does. I'm givin' you kids an' th' pup a ride.

It ain't allowed. Now, just in case we run into my super-
visor some place, I don't know. See? I'll kick yer back-
sides a little bit an' chase ya off . . . Okay?"

"Kick easy," Bob said.

"Sure," the driver said. "When's school open?"

"Few more days," Bob said, feeling talkative.

"Hell, ain't it!" the truck driver said. All in all he was
a very understanding person.

We gained speed. Bob and James and I felt around in
the stalks of bananas. Randolph sniffed. They were vivid
green; about as hard as ivory. But we were hungry. The
sun was straight up and then some. The graham crackers
had been used up a long time ago.

"Hey," the truck driver shouted over the roar of the
motor, "them bananas'll give ya the God-awfulest belly-
ache. Take my advice, leave 'em alone."

"We ain't et any," James yelled, shaking his head so
the driver could see it in the mirror and understand.

"But you been thinkin' about it!" he yelled back.

"How c'n he tell what we're thinkin'?" James asked
Bob and me in a whisper. Bob was over in one of the
forward corners, where he couldn't be seen in the mirror,
trying to locate a ripe banana.

"Get me one," I said softly.

"Me, too," James said.

James and I sat there in full view, playing with Randolph and looking innocent.

"S'no skin off my nose," shouted the truck driver.

"Only you kids don' know how bad it c'n be. Y' turn green, yer hair all falls out, an' yer toenails curl up. That is, if y' don't turn inside out completely!"

"What'd he say?" Bob asked. He'd heard. He just wanted confirmation.

"Inside out," the man continued. "From the bottom up, or from th' top down."

"I don't want any bananas," I whispered.

"Me, neither," Bob said.

"I *do!*" James insisted. "He jus' don't want us eatin' any. Get me one. That one you got your hand on. Get two. Th' one over there too."

Bob got them and concealed them in his shirt; then he crawled back and joined us.

The truck stopped once at a roadside grocery and the driver got Randolph some milk. Then we went on.

Then the truck slowed and stopped by the fork in the road that led to Mentor Marsh. We scrambled over the tail board and got out.

"All clear?"

We yelled that we were.

"Got th' pup out?"

We came around to the side of the cab and showed Randolph to the driver. He reached out and patted him and felt of his ears.

"Better carry 'im, if his feet hurt," he advised. "So long." He waved and started rolling.

"So long!" we yelled.

"Nice guy," Bob said.

"Gosh," James said. "I fergot th' fishin' line. I left it in th' truck."

"Not mine, you didn't," I said. "I got it right here in my pocket."

"Me, too," Bob said. "Here's th' bananas. They're like iron. You c'n watch us fish."

"I had it in my hand," James said, taking the bright green bananas and looking after the vanishing truck. "Doggone! I put it down 'cause it kept stickin' me."

"C'mon," Bob urged. "Shake a leg. It'll be two-thirty before we get to th' marsh. We'll only have about an hour to fish before we gotta start home."

We took the cut-off and went down a little dirt road with summer cottages and farmhouses set back on either side. Randolph struggled in my hands and insisted on being put down to smell things.

"I wish we lived out here," I said.

Bob nodded.

"You want some of my banana?" James asked.

"Not me!" I said.

Bob said something to James in telepathy.

"A-a-a-a, he was tryin' ta scare us," James replied, turning one of the rigid bananas in his hands, examining it.

"Throw it away," I recommended. "Put both of 'em in one of th' mail boxes an' surprise somebody." Galvanised iron mail boxes lined the sides of the rural road, each on its individual post. Some were in brackets of two. Randolph scurried from one side of the road to the other. He liked the country.

"I'm gonna eat it!" James insisted, stubborn. And he did. We three stood in the middle of the road and watched while he chewed and swallowed. His face was all puckered up, but in the end he looked at us triumphantly. Randolph blinked and sneezed. He didn't ask for any.

"How about the other one?" I asked.

"I'm full," James said. Bob grinned. So did Randolph. James went to the next mail box along the road, opened the front, and threw the banana in. It clanged like the clapper in a bell.

Randolph barked a puppy bark and tore down the road after a big Persian tom that had emerged from some honeysuckle. We let him go. He couldn't run too fast, and he was going in the right direction. We followed. It was a great day to be nine years old, or—like the twins—eleven years old, or, for that matter, to be two months and three weeks old, like Randolph.

"I'll bet they're bitin' t'day," I said.

"I'll bet," Bob agreed.

"Wish I hadn't fergot my line," James said.

"You ain't gonna need it," Bob said.

James belched.

"See?" Bob said. "Maybe you better start back right now?"

"Nuts!" James said. "You guys're chicken. It was nourishin'!"

Randolph had vanished into a grape arbor way up

ahead, still after the tomcat. Now, suddenly, he yelped for help. The grapevines shook and shuddered and he yelped louder. In fact, it became a great wail—pain, distress, and anger.

We ran.

Bob led the way through the fence. It was barbed wire and tore a big hole in his pants. The grape leaves thrashed around furiously. We saw flashes of Randolph and something else boiling around under the leaves. He'd been ambushed.

Heedless, we closed in from three sides.

"Somethin's slaughterin' him!" yelled one of the twins. "Get him!"

Bob dove and missed. It was the Persian tom. He had Randolph, or Randolph had him; it was hard to tell. Anyhow, they flip-flopped over into the next row of grapes. I jerked out of my jacket and used it as a shield. Bits of fur were all over the place.

Just as I leaped, I saw a flash of something else coming at me through the grapevines. Then we met, head-on, James and I.

We just lay there, in the fallen vines, until Bob's voice penetrated through to us. I lurched up and, holding my head, went to his aid. He was down on the ground on top of something he'd captured with my jacket. It was bouncing around quite a bit—and yowling to high heaven.

"Help me, guy!" Bob gasped. "I can't turn loose!"

I let go of my head and helped him press down on the jacket. Not even the two of us could hold it.

"James!" I yelled, my head splitting. *"James!"*

"Huh?" a voice said from somewhere in the grape-vines.

"Help!" Bob yelled. "Help—quick!"

"My head," the voice said eloquently, and somehow stupidly; also there was a strong note of pain.

"Quick!" I yelled. Snake like, a spread and pronged paw had worked from under the jacket and was searching for something to lacerate. We struggled to avoid it.

James came stumbling through the vines. He got down and helped us. The Persian quit struggling for the moment, but kept up the evil yowls and low, threatening snarls.

"Where's Randolph?" I asked.

"Over there," Bob said. "What happened ta you guys?"

"He butted me," I said.

"My head!" James said, shaking it sadly.

We looked around for Randolph. He was sitting under a grapevine about forty feet away, regarding us with interest and neutrality. He was all through with the fight, except as a spectator.

"You all right, Randolph?" Bob asked.

Randolph got up and trotted another ten feet and sat under another grapevine. He licked his shoulder and belly. He licked so high up on his chest that he fell over backwards. He got up and looked at us and smiled. Then he withdrew another ten feet.

"What're we gonna do?" I asked. "We can't just lay here on top a cat all day. We gotta turn loose some time."

"I got to hold my head," James said.

"Hang on, you guys!" Bob said. "He gets loose an' we'll bleed ta death, he'll claw us so bad. He's madder'n a wet hen!"

"I *gotta* hold my head," James said. "*I gotta.* It's busted . . ."

"Look," I said, "le's see if we c'n get th' cat into one of th' mail boxes an' close it up. I gotta hold my head too."

We struggled and fought and got clawed a little bit, but we twisted the jacket into a sort of sack, with the tom snarling and spitting inside, and got to our feet. Then we manuevered ourselves out to the road. Working desperately, we forced the beast into one of the mail boxes and slammed the front shut before it could leap out at us. For a second there was a furious scratching and thumping, then we saw that the catch was going to hold. So did the tom. He quieted.

We continued on down the road, moving faster now, trying to put a little distance between ourselves and the trapped cat.

Randolph asked to be picked up. Bob took him. Randolph had scratches down his back and on his face and legs and belly. But he had cat fur in his mouth. He bristled and growled and looked back. James and I held our heads.

"You kids!" somebody yelled—a man's voice. "What'd you do to Trinidad?"

We looked around. We couldn't see anybody.

"*Where is he?*" the voice angrily demanded. "What'd you do to him?"

"Talkin' ta us?" Bob asked the wind. We kept going.
Randolph barked. We looked in that direction. A red-
faced man was standing in the door of a woodshed. He
had a big red nose and he was hopping mad.

"*What you been doin' in them grapes? Where's Trinidad?*"

"He chewed up our pup! I guess it was him," Bob
yelled. "We didn' eat none a' yer ole grapes."

"*There wasn't any grapes there to eat!*" James said. He
turned to me. "You see any? Any blood on my head?"

"No, uh-uh," I said, "I didn' look for grapes. Any on
mine?"

"Bet my skull's fractured," James said, groaning. "It
even hurts me ta blink my eyes!"

"Where's Trinidad?" the man demanded, advancing
toward the road. We kept going. "*Here, Trinidad! Here,
Trinidad! Here, Trinidad! Here, boy!* Where is he? *You
kill him?*"

"*Him?*" I shouted. "He almost kilt *us!*"

Randolph barked.

"*Come back here,*" the man yelled. "I'll have th' law
on ya! *Where's Trinidad?*" He was excited.

"I'm gonna tell 'im!" James said. The man had reached
the road and was starting after us.

"Sure, he deserves it!" Bob said. I agreed.

We stopped.

"Open yer mail box, mister," James shouted.

"What?" He shook his fist at us.

We walked backwards so that he wouldn't gain on us.
We were about three hundred feet up the road.

"Open th' *mail box*," I shouted.

"Ya deef?" Bob asked.

The man shook his fist some more. He was right in front of the mail box. He opened it.

It exploded. The tom came out just like a cannonball. It hit the man right on the chest and went straight up the front of him, over his face, right to the top of his head.

"*TRINIDAD!*" the man screamed. He didn't have any hair. He staggered back. "*TRINIDAD . . .*" he shrieked, beating at the air.

"*Jeez!*" Bob said.

"*Lookit his head!*" James gasped.

Randolph's neck hair stood on end.

The man ran back up the path to the woodshed, Trinidad still on his head and shoulders, spitting and raking.

We turned and ran.

We didn't stop until we were way out in the marsh and had found our boat. We emptied the water out of it, launched it, got in, balanced everything just right, and paddled out. We'd brought worms from home—in our pockets.

We hadn't even gotten to the place where the big bull-heads lived when James said he wanted to go back in.

"What for?" I asked, impatient to start fishing.

"My head hurts," James said weakly. "Anyhow, I ain't got my line."

"Won't feel any better on land," I argued.

"My head hurts so bad I got a pain in my stumik,"

James said. His belly rumbled. Randolph cocked his head at the sound.

"That banana!" Bob said.

We paddled back and put James ashore; then we paddled back out again. James went into the high reeds and turned inside out, just as the truck driver had predicted, only both ends at the same time. We could hear him doing it all the way out on the water. Randolph didn't like it. He growled.

We caught bullheads such as we'd never caught before. We lost all track of time. We caught about forty. The sun was getting low when I noticed it. We'd used up our worms, except for those on our hooks, and the mosquitoes were beginning to make noises.

"Hey," I said, "Bob, we better be gettin' back. It must be five o'clock. If we don't catch a ride right off, we'll be in for it!"

We paddled for shore. James was there. He was lying on one of the dunes that separated the marsh from Lake Erie. He was quite subdued.

"How you feel?" Bob asked.

"I'm empty, completely," James replied without even opening his eyes. "I'm so empty the skeeters don't even bite me."

"We gotta go home," I said, after Bob and I had hidden the boat. James feebly got to his feet. "You don't look so awful," I lied.

"Look swell!" Bob said. We were worried. We hadn't

seen him close up since we'd put him ashore. From the sounds he'd made he seemed vigorous enough. Now it looked as if he wouldn't even be able to make it up to the highway.

"I'm hungry," James said. "I'm so hungry I could eat wax paper or wet cardboard, I could." A tinge of color came back into his face. He was all right.

"You want a banana?" Bob asked.

James ignored him.

Randolph bounced around in the sand, growling at the string of fish, happy to be ashore where he could smell things again.

We were out of the marsh and at the beginning of the graded road when we met two kids on bicycles; they were about our own age. They looked shaken. Randolph growled and got between my legs.

"Hello," we said.

"Hello," they said. "You guys goin' that way?"

"Yeah," Bob said. "Why?"

"Crazy guy down there, got his head all tied up like a Egyptian!" one of the boys said. "Like a mummy. He's lookin' fer some kids. Fer a minit there he thought we was them. He's got a big stick."

"Yeah?" James sat down.

"He let us go," the boy continued. "He's waitin' fer th' other guys. He said they gotta come back that way sooner or later."

"He said he was gonna cane 'em within a inch a' their

lives!" the other boy continued. "Then he's gonna call th' cops. They had a dog along 'at almost killed his tom cat. Druv it crazy, he said. You them? That li'l ole dog the dog?"

"They was 'vandals'—ruint his grapes, he said," the first boy resumed. "We hadda talk fast. You them?"

"We better go back an' fish some more," I said.

"Be seein' ya," Bob said.

We left the strangers and went back into the marsh.

We went down and sat on the dunes for about half an hour, then tried again. We sneaked up the road until we saw the man. He was sitting right out on the road, by the mail box, in a rocking chair. His head was all tied up, right down to his neck. So were his hands. We hid and watched. He rocked and rocked and rocked. Every minute or so he'd stop the rocking chair, look all around, and start again.

We crawled back far enough so that he wouldn't see us, then got up and ran for the marsh.

It began to get dark. We'd been up to the road four or five times by then. Once he spotted us and gave chase. He ran us all the way into the swamp. We lost him in the reeds. He didn't waste any time. He turned right around and ran back up to the road and the high ground so that we wouldn't be able to cut around behind him and get away. That's what we'd planned; it didn't work.

"Doggone ole Egyptian," James panted. "He sure c'n run!"

"He'll catch us sure if'n we try to pass by his place while it's light," I said.

It was all open country up there. There were houses every couple of hundred feet, on both sides of the road, and nothing but open fields in between. He could run faster than we could in deep grass. We'd already found that out. His legs were longer. "We gotta wait till after it gets dark."

"You know what's gonna happen when we get home, huh?" Bob asked in telepathy.

"Sure," James said aloud, dispirited, nodding at me. "His mom's gonna be over at our house sittin' in th' livin' room talkin' with Mom an' Pop. Pop's gonna take us out to th' garage. An' him too."

"She's gonna say she isn't strong enough," I agreed, biting my lip.

That wasn't as demoralizing as it sounds. It knit us into a tighter unit. We were in the same spot and were going to suffer the same tortures.

We became more daring. We made another attempt. The man almost caught us He almost kicked a hole in James. It was an accident. It was dark by that time.

We tried to creep past the rocking chair, wiggling along on our stomachs in the ditch on the opposite side of the road. We were just opposite the chair and it looked as if we were going to make it, when suddenly we saw the man standing over us, head swathed in white bandages. Randolph gave us warning. He wuffed. We took one look. Then we got up and ran for all we were worth.

Bob threw away our forty bullheads so that he could run faster. The man grabbed hold of my jacket. I ran right out of it.

James was carrying Randolph. He stumbled and dropped him. Randolph rolled along the ground right in front of James and the man. They were so close that the man was almost touching James and James was almost touching Randolph, both of them bent over, each trying to grab hold.

Randolph stopped rolling and James dropped down to get him. The man couldn't stop that quick. His foot caught James in the ribs and he took a header into the ditch. He didn't get up right away. Neither did James. We ran back, got James and Randolph. I couldn't find my jacket in the dark, and hurried them back to the refuge of the marsh.

"What're we gonna do now?" I asked when we were safe in the dunes.

"I dunno," James panted, sitting down and holding his ribs. "On'y jus' count me out!"

"Ya did 'at keen!" Bob said, pleased. "D'ja hear 'at guy when he lit on his head?"

We sat down on the sand and grinned at one another, breathless. I picked up Randolph and patted him. The moon was coming up.

"Did ut on purpose!" James lied, feeling better.

"Lost my jacket," I said.

"Betcha he goes in th' house an' locks th' door," Bob said, looking out over the calm lake.

"Randolph's hungry," I said. "His stumik's makin' empty noises. We gotta get him home."

"We c'n pull out pretty soon," Bob said.

"Out around back, through the fields," I suggested. "He'll never see us out there at night." The moon had come up and was making patterns on the water.

"Right up th' road," Bob said. "In twen'y minutes 'at guy'll be in bed. An' he done it all ta hisself!"

We chuckled together.

Then Randolph stiffened and peered into the dark. I grabbed his mouth and held it shut. His cheeks puffed up, but the bark couldn't get out. We flattened. Someone was coming. James got alarmed and started to get up to run. Bob tripped him and held him down. We were in a cup in the dunes, perfectly concealed—and able to see just about everything, all around.

"*Keep still,*" I whispered. "*He'll never find us.*"

"Sh-sh-sh-sh—" Bob warned.

We watched and saw a white form come down the path through the bullrushes.

"*Got 'is whole body in a sling!*" Bob whispered, unable to keep the thought to himself.

Up on the high ground we could see lights in windows. The figure came closer. It passed within a few yards of us. It was a girl—maybe fourteen or fifteen. She was wearing a white bathrobe and her hair was in two braids. It was black. So were her eyes. And her face was very white and very beautiful. Possibly the moonlight had something to do with it.

We kept quiet.

The girl went down to the water's edge. She stood there for an instant, looking out over the vast lake. She was slender.

She listened. She turned, looked up and down the beach, paused, then, satisfied that she was alone, took off her robe.

James caught his breath. Bob squeezed my arm. My heart beat.

The girl bent and placed the folded robe on the sand, lay something on it, then turned and walked out into the lake. She lowered herself into the water until only her head showed, then swam, smoothly and swiftly, straight out—about a hundred yards—then straight back.

Then she was standing on the beach again, a few short yards from us. She squeegeed the water from her body with her hands, then bent and wrung the water from her braids. She dried herself with a towel, but she didn't put on the robe. Instead, she took up the shadow that had lain there. It was a violin. The moon glistened on the polished wood. The girl took up the bow. Bow in one hand, violin in the other, she turned from us and looked out upon the lake. She took two steps toward it. Toes in the dark water, back to us, she bowed—very slightly and very gracefully. She straightened. Waited an instant. Put the violin to her chin, lifted the bow—and began.

Then, much later, the violin silent, she bowed again, then again. She would have departed, but the silent ovation she received from the lake would not allow it; there had to be an encore.

And there was.

Then, when it was done, she tore herself away from her audience. She bowed, and bowed, and bowed, and laughing to herself put on the robe and fled up the path and disappeared.

We went up to the road and got to the highway without being chased. We didn't talk. I carried Randolph. He was sound asleep.

Some headlights came along. We stuck out our thumbs. The lights slowed, then stopped.

"Hey, you kids," a familiar voice called, "yer folks allow ya ta stay out like this?" It was the banana truck. "C'mon, hurry up," the friendly driver said. "Here, in front. Nobody'll see anythin' at night. Supervisors all home smoking their pipes an' kissin' their wives. Only us workin' stiffs out. How's th' pup?"

We piled in.

"He's awful hungry an' all scratched up," I said. "He didn' eat a thing all day, not since you gave him milk. We been in all kinds a' trouble. I lost my jacket."

"We're *in* all kinds a' trouble!" Bob corrected.

"Out so late . . ." James said.

The truck driver put the truck in high and we thundered down the highway.

"Tell me all about it," he said, *"everythin'*. How were those bananas? I'll get ya home in a jiff. Right ta yer front door, how's 'at?"

"You know about them bananas?" James asked.

"Hell, yes!" the man said, laughing.

We told him everything that had happened—except about the girl. James told him his version of the day's events. He left out the part about the girl and the violin. Bob didn't mention her either. The friendly truck driver had tears in his eyes, he'd laughed so much. He demanded that I tell him my version of what had happened. I also left out the important part. I didn't intend to. I was going to go James and Bob one better. But when I got to that part I stopped.

Mr. Scott was comparatively easy on us. The truck stopped right in front of the house and the driver came to the door with us. He told Mr. and Mrs. Scott and my mother that we'd had a lot of hard luck and so on and so forth. Mr. Scott smiled and thanked him for bringing us home. Then, as the truck roared away, he took us out to the garage. He used the razor strap I'd heard so much about.

>>><<<

The few days before school opened were musically frantic. The twins had fights about whose turn it was to

159

practice, or who was hogging the piano. I made thirty-five cents delivering suits and dresses for the dry-cleaner at the corner. I really made a dollar and a quarter, but I dropped a suit and dress in a gutter and stepped on them.

I blew the entire thirty-five cents on a mouth organ and played my lips raw before, fortunately, I lost it— about the same time that the twins decided that the piano wouldn't respond adequately. It wasn't that they didn't try. They almost wore themselves out and drove Mr. and Mrs. Scott insane with their trying. Randolph got inflamed eardrums and howled himself hoarse. He got so that he croaked just like a bullfrog.

And I sometimes think that my mother threw away the mouth organ. It didn't matter. Spiritually and intellectually our musical development was so far advanced that there wasn't any hope of our fingers or tongues ever catching up.

It was all thanks to Randolph. If he hadn't tackled Trinidad and gotten us into trouble we might never have awakened musically.

Anyhow, two weeks after school opened we were taken to the first concert. There might have been a little trouble. That possibility always existed, however remote. But not that day. There was a violin soloist. A virtuoso. A young girl.

The instant she walked on the stage and faced us our hearts leaped, then hushed. We didn't move a muscle all the while she played. She had black hair and she was beautiful—quite as lovely as she'd seemed by the lake.

She played Lalo's *Symphony Espagnole*. Then, when we demanded an encore, she lifted the fiddle, smiled, and played, as she had before, *Spanish Dance* by Granados.

Bob and James and I weren't the same for days and days.

13

The End of Youth

WE DID all right in school that fall. I think it was Randolph's influence.

He thrived. He grew and grew. He ate everything. He even ate cucumbers and tomatoes—anything he saw us eat. Once he chased a cat up a tree and the Fire Department had to get him down. The firemen accused us of putting him up there. We hadn't. Randolph was just impetuous.

James and Bob and I wanted to be fair, but we had a few heated discussions about how to divide Randolph's time. They wanted him to sleep three nights at their house and one at mine. I argued that it wasn't right! It wasn't my fault they'd been born double, or that Babe was their kid brother—and I didn't want to be penalized! Randolph decided it in my favor. He slept with me every other night. He had one ear that stood up and one that wouldn't and was inside-out most of the time. His legs were too short for his body and that gave the impression that he was longer than he really was. But he had a great personality.

We grew up suddenly. In two days. Randolph, too. Winter came on. We fought it as long as we could. For a long time we went swimming just as though it was summer. Randolph couldn't take it. He got so that he'd watch us from the bank. Even looking made him shiver.

Then, at the end of October, indigo and shuddering, so chilled that we could hardly move our knee joints, we had to admit defeat. We were still children then. The two days in which we were to attain worldly wisdom hadn't yet arrived. But they were drawing nearer.

Afternoons, after we got out of school, old men with rakes would be standing out in front of their houses talking to one another and watching piled-up leaves smoulder. There was a vast, painful melancholy in the blue smoke drifting up through the naked branches. And the pungent aroma was enough to break a boy's heart. Summer had perished. We felt age creeping up on us. And there was nothing we could do. We even got to worrying about the future.

Then, one day, while we were in class, the sky got so overcast and the world so dark that the janitor turned on the lights. Then George Hopper pointed—and we saw the first snowflakes feathering down.

Real snow came and we wore galoshes and windbreakers

and our toes froze and we got cold just the same. We got Flexible Flyers for Christmas. Lake Erie turned into a solid sheet of ice that extended miles and miles out from shore.

In the mornings I used to slick my hair down with water. It was frozen stiff by the time I got to school. I did it to show how rugged I was.

It became so cold that the twins and I had to postpone getting into fights until it got a little warmer. It hurt something terrific to hit a guy in the eye with a cold fist. It was just like jumping off a fence when your feet were cold, and landing flat-footed. It was something you'd never do twice, not voluntarily.

Then, right after my birthday—we'd advanced into 6A—the two days arrived. We lost our youth. Randolph led us into love. He almost broke up the secret society, just when it was at its peak.

First, the Coffees moved away.

Bert and Jimmy came to say good-bye. The twins and I were shoveling snow out of our clubhouse. Randolph and Babe and Myrtle were up on top, watching.

Randolph was the first to spot the approaching Coffees. Myrtle was second. Randolph barked his angry bark; he had all kinds.

"Ho, ho," Myrtle said. "Ho, ho, here *they* come!"

She and Babe ran around to the far side of the clubhouse, putting the excavation between the Coffees and themselves. Randolph stood his ground, growling.

"Hey, quick," I told the twins, after a look, "here come Bert an' Jimmy. Make snowballs. Hard ones!"

James and Bob stuck their heads over the top to see how much time they had, then dropped down and feverishly started making snowballs. Randolph sensed the emergency. He advanced one step toward Bert and Jimmy, stiff-legged, teeth bared. They stopped. Their hands were empty.

"You guys . . ." Bert called. "Ya want our clubhouse? We're movin' away."

"Beat it," I suggested. One of the twins handed me two solid snowballs. "Scram—this here's our territory!"

"Aw, dry up," Jimmy said, keeping an eye on Randolph. He made a feint as though he was going to throw something. Randolph didn't scare. He flattened close to the snow and began a steady advance on the Coffees, ears against his head, eyes narrowed, teeth glistening. Bert and Jimmy backed up. I called to Randolph to stop. He obeyed reluctantly, sinking down on the snow, eyes never leaving the enemy.

"We didn' come over ta fight!" Bert told us. "Want our tree house, or not? It's got a roof, an' a floor, an' walls—an' no snow or mud in it!"

"Even got a stove," Jimmy added. "See three blocks every which way from up there. Nobody c'n surprise ya."

"C'n see inta th' McCutchin's bathroom," Bert said. "Every Saturday night all the McCutchin girls take a bath. Want it, huh?"

Armed, James and Bob and I crawled up out of the dugout. We could see the tree house up in a big elm that stood in another empty lot about two blocks away. It was a hut made of two piano boxes that had been hoisted up in sections and hammered together.

"What's th' catch?" I asked.

"Nothin'," Bert said. He and Jimmy tried to come closer. Randolph lifted himself from the snow and took another stiff-legged step toward them. He was rigid with hostility. His tail stuck straight out behind him and it trembled with rage.

"Stay right where ya are!" James warned. "We'll sic him on ya . . ." We held our snowballs ready. Each had a rock inside.

They stopped.

"Well," Bert demanded, "want it?"

"We're movin' down ta 105th Street," Jimmy boasted, sneering, "close by *Keith's RKO*. Our old man's been transferred. We're gonna see vaudeville every day! We gotta give our tree house ta somebody. Want it?"

"When ya goin'?" Babe yelled.

"Yeah—ho, ho?" Myrtle echoed.

"T'day," Bert said.

"We're all moved," Jimmy said. "House stuff's all gone. We ain't never gonna see you guys any more. Want it? If ya don't, we'll bust it up."

Myrtle picked up her dress and blew her nose in her petticoat.

"Cryin'?" Babe asked. "Wuffor?"

"Never see 'em again," Myrtle said into her petticoat. It was sort of tragic. Even losing enemies was painful.

"Honest, leavin'?" Bob asked.

"Right away," Bert said. "Want it?"

"Yeah—sure—we want it," I said. "Heck, yes!"

"What time they take a bath?" James asked.

"Before goin' ta bed, late," Jimmy said. "Two at a time. They never pull the shade down. They don't know we c'n see in."

"See good?" Bob asked.

"*Perfect!*" Bert said. "Even see th' plug in th' bottom of th' bathtub while they're gettin' out an' gettin' in— till the little kids make th' water too dirty. They're last. So long, you guys."

"Yeah, so long," Jimmy said.

We all said so long and they went away. It was all over. We relaxed. Randolph sat down on the snow and watched them go. Babe kicked some snow into the clubhouse. We didn't tell him not to.

"Le's go down an' slide on th' lake," I suggested.

Randolph took a last look up the street, got up, shook himself, and looked at us in the way that meant let's go. He liked sliding on the ice. He liked everything we liked.

"How about we go over an look at th' new clubhouse, huh?" Babe suggested.

"*After* they're gone," Bob said. "You an' Myrtle stay here an' see if they *really* go."

167

"Put yer dress down, Myrtle," Babe ordered; she was blowing her nose again. "I c'n see yer belly-button. Don't ya get cold?"

They stayed behind. We went down to the lake.

"Good riddance of bad rubbish!" James said.

Bob nodded.

"It's got a stove, he said," I recalled.

"I've seen smoke comin' out," James said.

We started out onto the lake. The ice was coarse and humped for about a quarter of a mile, then it turned into gravel, then sandpaper, then plate glass.

"We'll move in right away," James said.

"Wonder what the catch is?" I said.

"Me, too," James nodded.

"Nimi's th' oldest," Bob said, thinking of the Mc-Cutchins' bathroom window, "she's finishin' high school next year. Then there's Marvel, she's a year younger . . ."

"After Marvel comes Jerry. She's fourteen," James said. "I once saw her kissin' somebody on the porch swing. Then Morgie, she's prettiest . . ."

"She'd sure get mad if she found out about us seein' her nekkid in th' bathtub," Bob said, grinning. Morgie was in our class at Memorial.

"Pop's gonna beat th' stuffin' outa us fer bein' out late an' not comin' home Saturday nights," James said.

"After Morgie comes Vera an' Grace," I said.

"Then June an' Hope," James said.

"I'm only stayin' as far as Grace," Bob said, "we're gonna get kilt as it is."

We unanimously agreed that we'd leave when Grace got out of the tub. June and Hope didn't count; they were Babe's age.

"When's Saturday?" Bob asked.

"Three more days," I said.

"We gotta watch out fer Babe an' Myrtle," James warned. "Wait an' see! They'll make us give 'em all kinds a' stuff ta keep quiet. They heard everythin'."

"Where's Randolph?" I asked, suddenly missing him. We looked around. We didn't see him anywhere.

"Randolph!" I yelled. "*Ran—dolph!*"

All three of us yelled:

"*RAN—DOLPH!*"

"There he is!" James pointed. Randolph jumped up on a hummock of pressure ice close to the beach, barked joyously for us to come see what he'd found, and disappeared again.

"He's got somethin'," I said. "We better go see what it is."

We made haste slowly; the ice was slick.

"Girl over there . . ." Bob observed. "Got a sled."

"Mus' be somethin' else," James said, "Randolph don't like girls."

"Who does?" I asked.

"Exceptin' Mary Heaven," Bob reminded me.

169

"That's different," James said. "She's Indian."

We had just about gotten to where we'd seen Randolph, when a girl came around the piled-up ice floes and looked at us. She had Randolph in her arms and he liked it. She was dusky and beautiful. She had immense almond-shaped eyes. She was gypsy.

"He yours?" she asked, looking from one of us to the other with her great eyes. She had a voice like water flowing, bees buzzing, deep grass rustling . . .

"Yeah," we said, spellbound.

"Whose?" she asked. She babied Randolph, upside down in her arms, and he looked up at her with lovestruck eyes. He was utterly out of his mind. But so were we out of our minds.

"Ours," we said. "He belongs to all of us."

"He's about got his full growth," I said. "He's not a puppy any more."

"Gosh!" Bob said, apropos of nothing at all.

"What's your name?" James asked very gallantly.

"Tisa—I'm Tisa," the vision said. Randolph licked her under the chin. She laughed and squeezed him. Randolph hated being squeezed, but this time he enjoyed it. She looked at us again, eyes sparkling.

"He's kissing me," she said.

"Yes," we said weakly.

"I'm nine," she said.

"Me, too," I said quickly, feeling the bond between us strengthen. "They're goin' on twelve."

"So what?" James demanded. "Anyhow, you're ten now!"

"I like you, all . . ." Tisa's red lips said, just in time to forestall an incident. "Especially him." She hugged Randolph again.

"Jus' move here?" James asked tenderly.

"Yes," Tisa smiled, "we're gypsy."

"You're dressed like one," Bob mumbled, still dazed.

"It's a gorgeous dress!" I exclaimed, taking advantage of the break. "I always wanted to meet a gypsy."

"You," Bob said, ignoring me, looking Tisa right in the eyes, "are the most beautiful girl I ever saw!"

Tisa lowered her eyes and kissed Randolph on the top of his head. He almost swooned.

"Lemme pull you on th' sled," I said, picking up the rope.

"We'll all of us pull!" James declared, grabbing a hand-hold.

We towed Tisa and Randolph out onto the smooth ice. She kept Randolph in her arms.

"*Look*," I said, becoming enraged, "it was *my* idea!"

The twins ignored me. I jerked the rope out of their hands.

"*I'm* gonna do th' pullin'!" I declared.

"Yer loony!" James shouted, grabbing at the rope again.

"You got a girl!" Bob shouted.

"Sure!" James yelled. He turned to Tisa, spoke gently:

"He's got a girl named Mary Heaven in South Dakota.' She's Indian. They're gonna get married. They're already engaged!"

"I've been there," Tisa said to me, smiling.

"I'll bet I met you some place," I said. "We must've *at least* passed on th' highway. Think of it!"

"Pull, huh?" Tisa said.

"Sure," I said, and lunged against the rope and fell flat on my face.

"Goof!" James said. He and Bob took up the rope and started off with Tisa. I got to my feet as fast as I could Bob slipped and fell, but wouldn't turn the rope loose. I caught up.

"I'm gonna clip ya right in the mouth," I yelled at James.

"Clip me!" James dared, acting heroic for Tisa. Bob got up, slipped, and fell down again.

"*I will!*" I warned.

"Do it . . . I *dare* ya," James insisted. He didn't think I would. I cocked my hand and let him have it. His feet shot out from under him and hit mine. We thudded down on the ice. Wrestling and hitting at each other, we panted and struggled around on the ice until we had to acknowledge that fighting in this temperature was too painful. Then we heard Randolph barking way off in the distance. Bob had hauled the sled away.

It was a strenuous, exciting, and frustrating day. Tisa wouldn't show any partiality. Before evening and parting she told us that she loved us. She loved us individually—

and collectively. She loved Randolph especially. She kissed us good-bye, right on the lips.

I couldn't eat any dinner.

The next day was worse.

The Coffees actually had gone. We met Tisa and took her up into the tree house. Randolph followed. We'd left him at the foot of the trunk, with Myrtle and Babe. Gasping and trembling, Randolph crawled up the board rungs and joined us. Myrtle and Babe were afraid to. Randolph didn't like height, not when he stopped to give it any thought, but he was sold on Tisa.

We kindled a fire in the five-gallon can that Bert and Jimmy had made into a stove. It was dark and cozy and wonderful in the tree house. There weren't any windows, only little lookout holes that had been bored with an augur.

Tisa squeezed out of her coat and we could see her better. She got a mirror out of her pocket and made Bob hold it for her while she smoothed her hair. She had bracelets on her wrists and rings on her fingers and tiny earrings in her ears. She made us weak all over.

"Lord!" Bob said. "Tisa, marry me, huh?"

"Marry *me*," James said, anxious. "I'm gonna be more successful."

"I've got two-bits . . ." I said, for lack of anything else to say.

Tisa turned and looked at me with her beautiful eyes. She smiled.

"You go out . . ." she said to the twins.

"All three of us?" James asked.

"You two," murmured Tisa.

"Where? How far? How long?" James asked, hating me. My heart was pounding. *"Why?"* James demanded. "We got two-bits each, too. All of us been shovelin' walks."

"I want to tell a secret," Tisa said, pointing at me. "Him first. I'll tell you after I tell him."

"Promise?" Bob asked.

Tisa crossed her heart. She was utterly captivating.

"How far we gotta go?" James demanded gracelessly.

"Up the limbs—where you can't see in," said Tisa, pouting. She caressed Randolph and he fell over on his back.

The twins glared at me and squeezed out of the little door.

Tisa took Randolph in her arms, placing him before her in her lap. She put a few more twigs into the glowing stove. Then she looked at me. Then we kissed. I felt faint.

"I want candy," Tisa whispered into my ear.

"I love you . . ." I whispered guiltily, *"but I'm gonna marry Mary Heaven. She's Sioux. I promised."* I kept my two-bits in my pocket.

"What're they whisperin'?" James asked, outside.

"Can't hear," Bob replied.

"GO HIGHER!" Tisa commanded, speaking imperiously to the ceiling of the piano boxes. She changed. She looked positively wicked. Even Randolph noticed. He

174

looked worried. "GO HIGHER. *HIGHER!*" she shrieked. "If you listen I won't tell you later!"

"Tisa," I said. "It's dangerous. In the winter th' branches get brittle . . ."

She looked at me again. She puckered up her lips. The tree house shook and creaked as the twins climbed higher.

"Hey," Babe yelled from the foot of the trunk. "Whatcha doin'?"

"Lookin' fer enemies," James replied. "Tisa, hurry up, we're freezin'."

Tisa and I separated.

"Want to kiss me again?" Tisa asked softly.

"Uhuh," I said, unable to form words.

We did. Blinding little explosions were going off inside of my eyeballs and I couldn't get my breath.

"*Give me the money,*" Tisa whispered.

"*No,*" I whispered, "*it's all I got.*"

Tisa's eyes hardened for a fleeting instant. Then she softened again. It happened so swiftly that I thought I'd imagined it.

"*Want me to shimmy?*" Tisa whispered, looking naughty. My ears got hot. I nodded.

"*Give me money,*" she put out her hand. I fished the quarter out of my pocket and gave it to her. "*Watch!*" she whispered. She held her hands up in front of her and shimmied. The whole piano box shook. But something was wrong. Something had happened. She wasn't the Tisa I'd been in love with. She was a stranger.

175

"Now you go out," she commanded aloud. I stood up and bumped my head against the ceiling.

"Tisa," I said, hesitant, "you're not gonna shimmy fer them? You're not, huh?"

She put my two-bits in her stocking and worked it down her leg into her shoe. She ignored me.

"*Don't,*" I begged, "*please, Tisa . . .*"

Tisa looked up. She was pouting again.

"Hey," James said, "we're comin' down. We're froze!" The tree shook.

"Shimmy again," I urged, "before they get here!" She shook her head.

"Tisa," I said.

"No!" she said, scowling. "Not till you get me candy."

"You got all my money!" I protested.

"Get more," Tisa said, turning up her nose.

"You're not as pretty as I thought," I said. "You're a bad girl!"

"Ha-ha-ha," she laughed, but it was artificial; she was mad. She made her fingers into claws and threatened to scratch me. Randolph looked at her, incredulous. He stiffened and got to his feet.

The twins squeezed in the tiny door on their hands and knees. They were red from the cold. Tisa put out her hands and patted them on the cheeks just as though they were dogs—and they loved it.

"Tell us the secret," James begged of Tisa. He blew on his fingers.

"Whatcha do?" Bob asked, looking from one of us to the other.

"Nothin'," I said.

"You go out, now!" Tisa ordered.

"I'm goin'," I said. "You couldn' keep me!"

"What's wrong with him?" James asked.

Tisa wrinkled her nose.

"C'mon, Randolph," I said. He was ready to go. He didn't love Tisa any more. I got him under my arm and crawled out and got on the ladder. About two-thirds of the way down, I missed a rung and we fell the rest of the way. I landed flat on my back. Myrtle and Babe got clear just in time.

"Hurt yerself?" Babe asked, looking down at me. Randolph kiyied around the lot, then composed himself and came back and looked at me.

"No," I gasped, getting my breath.

"What ya doin' ta Randolph?" demanded a voice in the tree house, but didn't bother to look out.

"They fell part ways," Myrtle explained. "They ain't hurt."

I got up and moved away from the tree. We could hear whispering up above.

"What they sayin'?" Myrtle asked. "What you'n her do up there? *Kiss?*"

"Nothin'," I said.

The piano box shuddered. I didn't care. I even felt better. I knew that Bob and James were broke too.

I stood there with Babe and Myrtle. The tree house shuddered again.

"Kissin', I betcha!" Myrtle said.

According to my calculations they'd already done the kissing. What we were watching was the shimmy.

"Hey," Babe yelled, "kiss 'er fer me! Ho, ho, ho, ho . . ." He thought he was very funny.

"Shut up," I said, suddenly altruistic. "Leave 'em alone."

Randolph barked. We turned.

The old maiden lady who lived in the big house across the street was looking out her window, eyes fastened on the tree house. Randolph dashed across and barked at the window.

"How long Miss Mason been watchin'?" I asked.

"Long time," Myrtle said. "Alla time since you guys an' her clumb up in'a tree."

"*Lissen!*" Babe nudged me. "Her an' Bob an' James're fightin' up there!"

"BOB!" I shouted. "JAMES! Ole Miss Mason been watchin' us. We better get outa here!" Miss Mason didn't have anything better to do except get kids in the neighborhood in trouble. Run across her grass and she'd call the cops. And she was always telephoning somebody's folks. She hated Randolph. She liked cats. It was her cat he chased up in a tree that time. It got away, but it lost its mind.

There was some scuffling up in the piano-box hut. Someone yelled in pain.

"Fightin' a'right!" Myrtle said.

"Miss Mason," I warned again, "she . . ."

"*Looky!*" Myrtle shrieked, dancing away in terror. "*Th' house is movin'!*"

I looked. It had moved. I saw why. The nails had all been pulled out!

"*Look out! LOOK OUT!*" I howled. "THEM COFFEES PULLED ALL TH' NAILS!"

Randolph came tearing back across the street to get in on the new excitement. Myrtle and Babe squealed and jumped around on the snow. Alarmed by the sudden furor, Mrs. McCutchin and her eight daughters came pouring out of their house.

"*Get down!*" I yelled. "*GET DOWN, QUICK!*"

A head stuck out of the door. Then a shoulder. It was James's. He hadn't heard me. But he noticed the change in the position of the tree house. He couldn't reach the fork in the main trunk. And he didn't need a book of directions to tell him what was wrong.

"*Them Coffees!*" he screeched.

"What's happening up there? What you kids doin'? Why all the screaming?" Mrs. McCutchin screamed.

"Get down," I said to James. "*Quick.* Th' nails is out! They pulled' em out. Get down!"

"I can't!" he yelled, wide-eyed and desperate. "Tisa's holdin' on ta me. I wouldn' give her my money. She bit Bob!"

The piano box lurched. It creaked. There was a splitting sound. We all yelled. James was dragged back inside. He struggled out again. There was a thud. James grabbed at a twig that snapped off in his hand. He opened his mouth and yelled: "A-a-a-a-a-a-a-*a-a-a-a-a-a-a-a* . . ."

Mrs. McCutchin and her eight daughters, by this time with Babe and Myrtle and me, screamed with him—a deafening sound.

Then the tree house turned and toppled out of the tree.

It landed on one corner of the roof and burst. It was just like an explosion. Smoke and all. Boards sailed around and the stove scattered hot coals all over the place. And Mrs. McCutchin and her daughters were all over the lot, running to safety, running in, then running away again, screaming like mad.

James sprang out of the debris and dashed around the lot just as Randolph had.

"I got splinters!" he screeched. "I got splinters! I got SPLINTERS!"

Bob got to his feet slowly and stood in the center of the debris. There was smoke coming out of the top of his head, like a volcano. I ran into the welter and knocked the glowing ashes out of his hair.

"Holy Smoke!" he gasped. "Tisa bit me almost ta death!" He was on fire all over. Every time we'd put out one fire we'd discover another. Nimi McCutchin and Marvel and Jerry and Morgie helped put out the fires.

I looked for Tisa. She was about a block away and there wasn't anybody could have caught her, not even with a motorcycle.

Mrs. McCutchin and I corralled James, wild-eyed and tattered. June and Hope helped head him off. I grabbed hold of him.

"Lemme go!" he howled. "I got *splinters!*"

"Ole Miss Mason sure as hell telephoned our folks!" I said, hanging on to him. "We gotta get outa here! Ya got yer two-bits?"

James quieted long enough to feel in his pocket.

"Naw!" he howled, "naw—she got it. All I got is *splinters!*"

"Where?" Myrtle asked.

"*Everywhere!*" James yelled.

"What on earth were you doing up there?" asked Mrs. McCutchin.

"Lookin' in th' bathroom winda," Myrtle shrilled, starting to run. "They was lookin' in th' winda, watchin' th' girls take baths!"

"Two at a time!" Babe shrieked, joining her. "Nimi an' Marvel; th' big ones first. *Two at a time . . .*" He and Myrtle had gone temporarily crazy. The events of the last few minutes had been too much for them. They were unhinged enough to be capable of anything. They were getting back at us for all the frustrations we'd heaped upon them.

"*WHAT?*" cried Mrs. McCutchin.

"Satidy night, after supper!" Babe shrieked, hysterically happy, and running for all he was worth. "*Two at a time!*"

Then Mrs. Scott arrived.

ONE-DOG MAN

Miss Mason had telephoned.

Mrs. McCutchin and her daughters told Mrs. Scott we'd been peeping in the bathroom window! They didn't tell it; they screamed it!

We tried to defend ourselves. We said we hadn't, yet. It was only Friday.

Mr. McCutchin came home and waved his arms.

Mrs. Scott got mad at him and took our side, until she dragged us home.

Halfway, she suddenly cried:

"Where's Randolph?"

We stopped and looked around us, sick with apprehension.

"He went home when th' house blew up," Myrtle yelled from a block away, "I seen him!"

>※<

What with one thing and another, that day marked the end of our childhood.

Never again were we to be interested in girls who couldn't shimmy—or to trust them if they could.

Never again were we able to accept gifts out of season, not without wondering what the catch was.

So—innocence and trust went out of our lives.

What else is youth?

182

✳✳✳ *14* ✳✳✳

Desperation

MRS. EDDY graduated us from 6A and said
good-bye. Next Autumn we would go to Collinwood Junior High. We were grown-ups now, she said.
She gave us a little speech and said that she was mighty
proud of us and expected great things. She said that the
future lay before us and that she was happy that she'd
been privileged to accompany us part of the way. Then
she sat down and blew her nose.

We filed out of Memorial Grammar School for the last
time. Randolph was waiting in the schoolyard. He bounced
around with joy at the very sight of us. But we couldn't
respond.

We straggled out of the yard and started home. The
summer was ahead of us. But so was the future. We went
slowly, thinking. We didn't feel like grown-ups. And yet
neither did we feel youthful.

"I'm goin' on eleven," I said.

"We're almost thirteen," James said, understanding.

"Life's jus' flyin' away," Bob said, shaking his head and avoiding walking on the sidewalk open places, only stepping on the cracks and where the lines crossed.

Randolph got depressed and walked along at our heels; he hung his head and didn't bother to smell anything.

"Le's us never, never bust up, huh?" James said.

"Always stick together!" Bob said, brightening.

"Th' Three Musketeers!" James said.

"No matter what happens!" I said. "You're my *best* frie nds."

"Shake," Bob said, sticking out his hand.

We stopped and shook hands all around. Each of us got down and shook Randolph's paw. He took our hands solemnly.

Then we felt much better. At least there was something we could count on in this changing world. Randolph perked up when he saw that our hearts were lighter.

That night the axe fell.

We'd just finished supper.

We were having dessert.

My mother told me that we were going back to live with the Indians. First, the Seminole—in Florida.

I didn't say anything. I couldn't even breathe.

"Heavens!" she exclaimed. "Aren't you happy about it? You always wanted to travel again."

"What about Randolph?" I said.

184

DESPERATION

"He isn't only yours," she said. "The Scott boys own more of him than you do. They wouldn't want to part with him. See?"

"I don't want to travel," I said. *"I want to stay with Randolph!"*

"You don't mean that! Indians . . ."

"I do!" I said. *"I do!* I DO! *I DO! Heck with Indians!"*
She looked unhappy.

"I'm sorry," she said, "but we'll have to go."

"When?"

"Next week. I was keeping it as a surprise for you."
I didn't say anything. I got sick right at the table.

Then, in the middle of the night, I woke up with a stomach-ache and had to take castor oil.

In the morning I was pale and shaken. My mother didn't want to let me go out until I looked better. I talked her into it. I told her I felt fine. But I still had cramps in my stomach.

James and Bob and Babe and Randolph met me half-way. They'd been on their way over to my house to see why I hadn't shown up.

"What's wrong, guy? Ya sick?" Bob asked.

"We're goin' away," I said.

"What?" All three of them stopped still.
Randolph came over and leaned against my leg.

"Fer vacation?" Babe asked.

"No," I said.

"Comin' back? Huh?"

"We never do," I said.

"Jeez!" Bob said. We sat down on the curb. I hugged Randolph and put my face down on his neck. Babe started to bawl. I couldn't keep the tears back either.

"When ya goin'?" Bob gasped.

Randolph snuggled up to me, tight. I got my breath.

"Next week, she said."

"*Jeez!*"

I stopped crying.

"Maybe I won't!" I said. The cramps in my stomach eased.

"Huh?" James asked. He'd been speechless. He wiped his eyes with the back of his hand.

"I'll run away, I will!" I said. "Randolph an' me!"

"No, ya won't!" James declared. "He's our'n more'n he's yours. We got *three* shares in him!"

"You got on'y one," Babe said, scared, pulling at Randolph.

"I wouldn' run far," I said, hanging on.

"How far?" Bob asked.

"Mentor Marsh!" I said as the thought struck me. "Him an' me'll live in th' boat. You guys could see him whenever ya wanted to! We'd eat bullheads an' sleep in th' boat."

Babe shook his head, but James and Bob were getting interested. Bob nodded; he wanted to hear more.

"How long'd ya stay?" James asked.

"Till my mother says we'll keep on livin' here in

DESPERATION

Cleveland an' not go anywhere," I said. "If'n I was ta hide out a whole month, that'd wear her down!"

The twins stuck their tongues out of the corners of their mouths and thought it over; they even had the same mannerisms. Babe watched them. Randolph licked my hand.

"How about it?" I begged. "Lemme take him. I *gotta* have company."

✕✕✕ *15* ✕✕✕

$\mathcal{R}$*unaway*

R ANDOLPH and I pulled out on a Sunday morning.
I got my fishing line and put some matches in a
needle case I swiped out of the sewing basket. I told my
mother that James and Bob and I were going fishing—
for the last time.

"Where?" she asked.

"White Park," I lied. That wasn't far; and it was in
the opposite direction from Mentor Marsh.

"Be careful."

"I will," I replied.

"How long will you be gone?"

"Till about four o'clock," I lied again.

"Taking some lunch?"

"I made me some sandwiches," I showed her the paper
sack.

"So much?" The sack weighed about five pounds; it was full to the brim.

"Fer all of us—James, Bob, Randolph, Babe, an' me!"
She nodded, preoccupied. She had a lot of packing to do.
"You be careful!" she warned.

As Randolph and I went out I got a rolled-up Navajo blanket I'd cached under the back porch.

James and Bob and Babe were waiting for us in the clubhouse—the dugout. We didn't want their folks to see us together and figure out that it was a conspiracy. The twins and Babe weren't to know that I'd run away, or where I'd gone. They were dressed up for Sunday school. That's where they were supposed to be right now. They had a tablet and pencil for me.

We sat down in the hole.

"You could write in blood . . ." James suggested, offering me a pin.

"Uh-uh," I said, "I might get an infection."

I used the pencil. I wrote my mother, saying that I was running away, forever. Randolph and I, together! I was leaving the note in the club house for the twins to find and give to her.

James and Bob read as I wrote.

"Tell 'er yer gonna drown yerself!" James suggested. "That'll scare 'er!"

"Sure," Bob agreed, "make her suffer!"

"No," I said; I was feeling sad. "Uh-uh, I love her."

"Never mind," Babe said. "She was gonna take ya travelin', wasn' she?"

"I like travelin'," I said.

"Then why ya runnin' away?" James asked.

"On account I like you guys," I said. "And on account of him." I patted Randolph. He licked my face. "Ya wouldn' let me take him along ta Florida, huh?"

"*NO!*" they shouted together.

"Well," I said, feeling miserable, "that's why I'm runnin' away—so's we c'n stay here an' always be together."

"Ya ain't gonna double-cross us an' really run off ferever with him, are ya?" James demanded.

"Yeah?" Babe said, looking alarmed.

"Uh-uh," I said, and I was so homesick I could have died. "Where'd I go? I'll be out in th' marsh. You guys're comin' t'morrow, huh?"

Bob nodded.

"We'll give 'er th' note tonight," James said. "Then we'll hitch out t'morrow an' tell ya what she said."

"She'll cry," I said.

"Think so?" Babe asked, pleased.

"Sure, she loves me," I said.

They walked me over to the boulevard. When we got there they each gave me a dime. They didn't say anything, just gave it to me. It was the money they were supposed to have dropped in the collection basket at Sunday school.

They stood back while I went out in the road with Randolph. I stuck out my thumb and the first car that came along stopped. It was terrible how fast I could run away. The man opened the door and Randolph and I got in and the car started up. I looked back at the twins and Babe. They'd come out into the roadway. They stood there, looking after me, getting smaller and smaller. At last we went around a curve and I was alone in the world—with Randolph.

"Where you going—running away?" the man asked. He startled me.

"No, sir," I said. "I'm goin' fishin'!"

"All alone?"

"Randolph an' me, sir."

"His name *Randolph?*"

Randolph had his nose out the window and was smelling the wind. At the sound of his name he turned around and smiled at us, then stuck his nose out the window again and blew bubbles.

"Yes, sir."

"Well, I'll be—" said the man.

We rode along in silence for a minute or two. Then the man looked us over again.

He asked: "Why you running away?"

"We're goin' fishin', sir," I said. He made me nervous. "Out to Mentor Marsh. For bullheads."

"How long you gonna stay?"

191

"T'day—till this afternoon."

"That why you got all that food along? And the blanket?"

"It's a Navajo blanket. It's to sit on," I explained.

"What about that sack?"

"Randolph eats an awful lot," I said. I wished I hadn't told the man how far I was going; I wanted to get out before he could ask more questions.

"You got enough chow there for a campaign!" he said. "Why you running away?"

I nervously got a tomato out of the sack and pushed Randolph in the ribs. He turned around and sniffed it.

"Go on," I ordered, "eat it!" I held the other food under his mouth so that he wouldn't drip on the upholstery. Randolph made a face, but he ate it.

"See!" I said to the man.

"Well, I'll be!" he said again.

"You goin' as far as Mentor Marsh?" I asked. "If you're not, I better get out here an' . . . ."

"Past there," he said.

We rode along without saying anything for about five miles. The man kept looking at Randolph and me.

"What's your name?" he suddenly asked.

"James—Bob—McCutchin—" I stammered.

"Which one?"

"All of them. James Robert Sc—*McCutchin*."

"Where d'you live?"

Randolph pulled his head in, listened to the conversation

for a second, lost interest, licked me on the ear, and stuck his nose out into the wind again.

"He likes ridin' in a car," I said.

"Most dogs do," the man said. "Where d'you live?"

"In Cleveland here," I said. "We used ta live other places, but now we live here."

"It's gonna rain tonight," the man commented, leaning over the steering wheel and looking at the sky. "You better be getting home early."

"Yes, sir," I said. The sky did look funny. It had been getting darker all the time.

Randolph saw a cat and barked at it and the hair stood up all down his back.

"Doesn't like cats, eh?"

"Hates 'em," I said. I wondered what I'd do if it rained. "He once chased a cat up a tree. The Fire Department had to get him down."

"You mean the cat," the man said. "Dogs don't climb trees."

"Randolph did, sir," I said. I figured that I could turn the packing case upside down on a dry place and sleep inside. "He didn't stop to think. He was up there about an hour before they got him down. There were crowds of people. The cat got away."

The man shook his head and went back to driving.

After a few minutes tiny raindrops speckled the windshield. Randolph sneezed.

"See!" the man said. "You better stick with me. I'm

coming back this way after supper. You and Randolph can stay with us until then. I've got the *Plain Dealer* and all the funny pages in the back seat. Then I'll drive you home."

"It'll stop raining," I said.

"What about your folks?" the man said. "Your mother and father are gonna be worried when you don't come home tonight—and it raining and everything."

"I've only got a mother," I said. "My father died a long time ago."

"Got any brothers and sisters?"

"I had a sister," I said. "I can't remember her very well. I called her Dee Dearest. She died when I was little."

"Then think how your ma's gonna feel."

"I'll be home in time," I said.

"How old are you?"

"Goin' on eleven," I said. "Randolph's not quite a year. His birthday is this week."

It was thundering and pouring down rain when we got to the crossroad that led off to Mentor Marsh. The man didn't slow up.

Looking straight ahead, he yelled suddenly: *"James!— Bob!"*

The windows were closed. Randolph put his front feet on the dashboard and squinted his eyes and looked ahead through the raindrops. He didn't see anything. He jumped over into the back seat and looked out the rear window. Then he looked out both sides. I looked around too.

The man said: "I thought that was your name?"

"It is," I said. "You better stop. We get off here."

"Who were you looking for—who's *he* looking for, if that's your name?"

"You surprised us," I said, "saying it so loud. We get off here."

"Oh, no you don't," he said. "Not by a long shot! Not in this rain, you don't. My house is a few miles up. You can stay there until it stops."

A woman opened the house door and stood inside, out of the rain, waiting and smiling as we came up the driveway. It was raining cats and dogs. The man stopped the car.

"C'mon," he said. "Let's run for it."

He kissed the woman. She was young and pretty, and both of them turned and looked at us; she closed the door.

"His name is James—Bob—Sc-McCutchin!" he told her. "And *his* name is Randolph!"

I said hello. Randolph smiled.

"Well!" she said, pleasantly.

"Um-m-m-hm-m-m . . ." he said. "We met on the road. They're staying here until it stops raining."

Randolph shook himself.

"Whoa!" said the woman. "Don't we want to keep him on the back porch? It's nice and cozy."

"Please, ma'm," I said, edging toward the door, "he isn't used ta bein' kept outside. We better be goin' . . ."

"Not on your life!" the man said. "Ruth, these are guests. Let's have something hot. Cocoa, huh? Does Randolph like cocoa?"

"He likes most anythin'," I said.

"You aren't lying!" the man said. "You know," he told the pretty woman, "I personally saw him eat a tomato! And once he climbed a tree and the Fire Department had to put up ladders and get him down!"

"He was up there an hour," I added, "hangin' on for dear life."

"What'd I tell you?" the man said to his wife.

We had cocoa together: the man, the woman, Randolph, and I. They put a piece of ice in Randolph's to cool it a little, and a part of the Sunday paper, the classified ads, under it to keep it from getting on the rug. I told them that it wasn't necessary—that Randolph was very dainty with his food. He was. He didn't spill a drop.

"They might stay here tonight," the man said.

"We'll be gettin' along," I said. "Th' rain's lettin' up."

"It'll be muddy," the woman said.

"Bullheads bite good after a rain."

"So they do," said the man, nodding. "But it's still raining. If it doesn't stop you won't be able to do any fishing. Since you've run away from home, you won't want to go back with me tonight—in fact I might just cancel that drive and not go into town until tomorrow."

The woman he called Ruth still had the shadow of a smile on her lips, but she wasn't following us very well.

" 'Run away from home'? "

"Yes, from his mother. She's all alone now."

"Dick," said the woman to the man, "will ours run away?"

"Any number of times," said the man, nodding.

"Did you?"

"Any number of times."

"Do you have a little boy?" I asked.

"Not yet, but pretty soon," said the man, looking at the woman. "Son, or daughter, it's all the same to me."

The pretty woman smiled and looked at me.

"Please, sir, ma'm," I said to them, sliding out of my chair, "I think I've got to be goin'." Randolph had been resting. Now he got up and went to the door.

The woman asked me: "Where does he usually sleep?"

"One night with me . . ." I said. "One night with Bob an' . . ."

"James?" asked the man, lifting his eyebrows.

I opened my mouth and shut it again.

I opened the door and Randolph and I ran. It was still raining. We ran across the open fields. The man didn't follow us very far; it was too wet. The weeds soaked us. He kept shouting after us. Then I understood. I'd left our sandwiches and the Navajo blanket.

We didn't go back. I had a hand line in my pocket and the marsh wasn't too far away. We went across the fields

until we reached the shore of Lake Erie. I'd been able to
see it from the house. We went along the shore toward
Mentor Marsh. The rain stopped and the sun came out.
We were dry by the time we got there.

I found our boat, the packing case with the sheet-iron
bottom. It was half sunk. I got part of the water out of it
and tugged it up on the edge of the swamp and levered it
over onto its side and dumped out the remainder. Then I
turned it back over again so that the sun could dry out the
inside. Then Randolph and I went fishing.

I caught four big fat bullheads before sundown. I
gutted and skinned them with my penknife and made a
fire in some damp twigs. Everything was damp. And it
looked as if it was about to start raining again. I used up
all the matches I had in the needle case before I got a
decent fire going.

My appetite departed with the sun. I cooked the bullheads on a twig and fed all of them to Randolph.

The moon came up. I sat there in the smoke of the fire,
hugging Randolph, and wondering what my mother was
thinking. By now she had my note. If it hadn't been for
Randolph I wouldn't have been able to bear it. I was
overcome with homesickness.

Then someone *hallooed* from somewhere farther down the
lake shore. I recognized the voice.

I got Randolph into the boat and crawled over the side
and shoved away from the bank. I had to paddle slow. If
I paddled fast the packing case churned around in circles.

And I had to be careful not to turn it over. It was sluggish and waterlogged and top-heavy.

But by the time the man got to my fire I was out in the center of the marsh and hidden in the cattails. Even if he was to spot the box, which wasn't likely in the moon-light—it had weathered to the same color as the muddy marsh water and blended with the reeds—he wouldn't be able to see us. The sides were three feet out of the water.

He had the woman with him.

"He's been here, all right," he said. "That's his fire."

He turned a flashlight on the marsh reeds. Randolph wuffed softly; just puffed up his cheeks. "*Sh-h-h!*" I told him. We scrunched down and watched through a crack between two of the boards.

"Hey," the man called. The flashlight beam wandered around. "Come on back. You can stay with us. We'd like to have a little boy. We like Randolph too."

Randolph perked up his ear when he heard his name. "*Sh-h-h!*" I warned.

The flashlight beam searched all over the marsh.

"What *shall* we do?" the woman asked. "We *can't* leave him and the dog out here all night!"

"If they won't come out from wherever they're hiding, we can't do anything else but!" said the man. "Some-thing's happened to them to make them run away. They don't want to go back. I guess they'll be all right until morning."

"But it's going to rain!"

"Hey," the man shouted. "Come on out. You can stay with us."

He waited. We kept quiet.

"Well," he called, "we're going home. I'm leaving you something to eat, here. And my raincoat. You'll be lonely. If you want to come live with us—you know where our house is. We'll keep the garden light and front-door light on all night. If you want to go home, we'll take you there. We've got a nice bed for you and Randolph."

Randolph wuffed. I grabbed him.

"Did you hear that?" the woman asked.

"Out in the water!"

"Yes . . ."

The light raked the reeds.

"See anything?"

"Nope."

"Listen," the man said, loud, "are you two all wet out there? I'm coming after you if you are." He started to unhook his raincoat. Suddenly he put his hands to his mouth and cupped them. "*RANDOLPH!*"

Randolph couldn't help himself. He had to bark.

"They're out there, Ruth!"

"We ain't wet," I yelled. "We're in a box."

"Well, come on back."

"No!" I said.

"The mosquitoes will eat you up," the woman said.

"We don't care."

"Don't you want to go home?"

"No."

"Why not?"

"My mom jus' wants ta . . ." I stopped myself.

"Yes, honey?"

"She wants to take me travelin'," I blurted. The "honey" did it. "We were goin' away an' leave Randolph an' never see him again, that's what!"

"Oh, *no!*"

"Yes, we was—we were," I said, "so we run off."

"I don't blame him, Ruth!" the man said.

"Shut up, you," she said. "He can probably hear every word we say." She called to me again.

"Honey, where are you? Come back here. Let's go home to my house and talk it over."

"No."

"He knows his own mind," the man said.

"*Please* . . ."

"No!"

"They must be in a submarine," the man said, throwing the flashlight beam around. "Let me talk to him.

"Tell us all about it. Why won't she take the dog? What'd she have against him?"

"She likes him," I said. "Everybody likes him."

"Jesus!" the man said.

"Well, then . . ." the woman said.

"She'd take him along. She says she wouldn't, but she would. But I only own one share of him." Tears started coming out of my eyes. Randolph licked them off my cheeks. I choked up. He whined.

"He's crying," the man said.

"Me, too," the woman said.

"God Almighty," the man said, "he eats tomatoes and climbs trees and people own stock in him!" He flashed the light over us again. "I tell you they got a submarine out there and 're talking to us through the periscope!"

"We got a box!" I yelled, sobbing.

"Okay, I believe you. What about Randolph?"

"I only own one share," I wailed.

"Who owns the others?" Ruth asked, she really was crying.

"James an' Bob an' . . ."

"*Them again!*" the man said.

"They won't let me have him."

"Why not?"

"They love him too."

"O my God," the man said.

I put my head down in my arms and wept. Then a frog or something plunked in the water and Randolph got up on his hind legs and looked over the side. I didn't notice until too late. The box slumped over and water rushed in; it disappeared beneath us. The man jumped into the water as he heard me yell. Randolph and I met him halfway.

"We can swim," I said.

"I wish you'd said so," the man said.

I told them all about Randolph as we walked the mile

or so to the road where their automobile was parked. Automobiles couldn't come all the way into the marsh, not after a rain. I told them how James and Bob and I had planned to make my mother stay in Cleveland. I told them all about the Coffee boys and how we got Randolph. I spilled over.

By the time we got to the house it was eleven o'clock. The man took a bath. The pretty woman helped me get out of my wet clothes—until she saw I was embarrassed. I kept my BVD's on. Then it was my turn to take a bath. While I washed myself the woman asked my name and address. I told her. We spoke through the partly open bathroom door. She kept her back to me. I told her about Indians. The Hopi and Zuni and Navajo were the cleverest with their hands; the Apache and Yaqui were the shyest; the Six Nations were the smartest with their heads; and the Sioux were the noblest. I told her the Sioux word for soap. I talked and talked and talked, reaction from being so alone in the swamp, so homesick.

I put on a pair of the man's pajamas that had been laid out for me. They were pretty large, but they felt better than the muddy, sodden clothing I'd shed.

I went out.

Ruth was sitting in the hall by the bathroom door, rubbing Randolph with a towel.

"Come on out to the kitchen," she said. "Let's be comfortable. I'll make something to eat."

"Where's the man?" I asked.

"Dick's gone," she said.

"Where?" I asked. But I knew where. We'd been betrayed.

We didn't try to run away. We just sat there in the kitchen, Randolph and I, getting sleepier and sleepier. Ruth watched us. She didn't have to. Our spirit was broken.

Randolph sat on a chair next to mine and I kept my arm around him. The woman, Ruth, gave us warm milk and cookies. She started to put Randolph's dish on the floor. She changed her mind and he ate from the table, with me. I gave him all of my cookies. I couldn't swallow very easy. And I wanted him to have nice memories of me.

Then, I don't know what time it was, Randolph wuffed and I heard car doors closing—and voices. Mr. Scott's voice, and the man's, and Mrs. Scott—and my mother.

They took Randolph and me home. James and Bob and Babe were in the back seat, sound asleep. The entire Scott family had been over at our house when the man showed up and told them where I was.

The twins and Babe didn't wake up when Randolph and I got in the back of the car. We went to sleep too.

>※<

My mother packed all the next day. I went over to see James and Bob. They weren't home. Mrs. Scott said they'd taken Randolph and Babe for a hike. I knew why. They didn't want to see me. They didn't want me to ask for Randolph. I was going away tomorrow and already we were strangers.

I went over and sat in the clubhouse. I sat there pretty nearly all day, all by myself.

Then the twins and Babe came home. When they saw me approaching they dragged Randolph into the house and locked the screen door.

I said: "I only came over ta say good-bye. We're leavin' in th' mornin'."

The twins blocked the door, standing shoulder to shoulder; Babe blocked out the lower part. Randolph and I couldn't see each other very well.

"When?" Bob asked. "What time?"

"Early, I guess," I said. "They're comin' an' takin' most of our stuff t'day. All except what we're takin' with us in th' car."

We stood there a second—not saying anything.

"Good-bye," I said.

"Good-bye," James said.

Bob shut the door.

I went home.

✖✖✖ *16* ✖✖✖

Love

JAMES showed up out in front of our house about six-thirty in the morning. The car was loaded and I was crying. James had Randolph along with him, on a rope.

"Hello," I said.

"Hi," he said.

I got down and put my arms around Randolph. I asked: "Come ta say good-bye again?"

"Yeah."

"Where's Bob?"

"He didn' wanta come. Babe either. They don' like sayin' good-bye. I brung Randolph."

"Thanks," I choked. "I was wantin' ta say good-bye t' him."

James bit his lip.

"Ya don't have to," he said. "He loves you more'n

he loves us. He whined all night. He knew you was goin'
away."

"Huh?" I said.

"You c'n have him," James said, scratching his forehead so that I couldn't see his eyes. "You ain't got a
brother." He turned and ran.

✳✳ *17* ✳✳

For Ever and Ever, Amen

RANDOLPH taught me many things. He taught me courage. And industry. And humor. And patience.

Once he sat for an entire week looking down a drain pipe. I had to take him his meals. I looked too. I couldn't see anything.

We traveled all over America. We ran over Pennsylvania's rolling hills and searched the plowed fields for flint arrowheads. We hunted skunks and baby alligators in the Everglades' cobwebby, mosquito-clouded aisles. We sat on Cochise Peak, just the two of us, and smelled the wind come out of Mexico. There were days in those years when the air was more delicious than perfume, more nourishing than any food.

I grew up. Randolph grew older.

He watched with pride as I learned to fly. That was

in Phoenix. He'd sit with his back against the hangar
office wall and watch me practice take-offs and landings;
then aerobatics.

One day after I got my license (he was no fool), he
trotted up to the plane, bracing himself against the prop
blast, and asked to go along. After that we flew together.
He had his own special flying harness that clipped to my
parachute harness. That was so that he wouldn't go sailing
out if we hit a bump—and so that we could jump together
if ever we got into any trouble.

We never drew apart. We always had time for each
other. He never once grew impatient with me, and I can
think of little to regret.

At last he passed away. He didn't suffer much. He was
feeble for a few days. I stayed with him. Then, in the
quiet of the night, I heard him stir. I woke up. I put my
hand over the side of the bed and patted him. He'd half-
risen; something had startled him. He licked my hand
and lay down again. I tried to go back to sleep. I couldn't.
I got up and turned on the light and took a look at him.
His heart had stopped beating.

That's fifteen years ago. I knelt beside him for quite a
while—until I was sure he was gone. Then I got up and
got dressed. I walked out to the airport. It was about
four miles. When I got there some Army P12's were
taking off in the dark dawning.

I went into the open hangar and found my plane. I

got into the cockpit and sat there. In a little while Kelly—
he lived over the office—came around with a flashlight and
asked who was there. I told him it was I. He asked what
was wrong? I told him Randolph had passed away.

Randolph was dead.